"We've got to s
onto his screen aft

"And meet in real life?" Ken typed eagerly.

The moment he hit enter, Ken realized the enormity of what he'd done. He wanted to hold Freeverse, to kiss her for real. What if she didn't want to? Or worse, what if they met in person and the cyberspark had flickered out? He held his breath and waited.

Apparently Freeverse was feeling the same doubts. "What if meeting in person means the end for us?" she asked.

"I hope it doesn't, but it seems like we've got to find out sooner or later," he said. "Do you really think it will be totally different, talking face-to-face?"

"I don't know," she said. "But I guess it's time to try. We have to know if this is for real."

MYSTERY
DATE

**Written by
Kate William**

**Created by
FRANCINE PASCAL**

BANTAM BOOKS
NEW YORK · TORONTO · LONDON · SYDNEY · AUCKLAND

MYSTERY DATE
A BANTAM BOOK : 0 553 506684

Originally published in U.S.A. by Bantam Books

First publication in Great Britain

PRINTING HISTORY
Bantam edition published 1998

Conceived by Francine Pascal

Produced by Daniel Weiss Associates, Inc,
33 West 17th Street, New York, NY 10011

Bantam Books are published by Transworld Publishers Ltd,
61–63 Uxbridge Road, London W5 5SA,
in Australia by Transworld Publishers (Australia) Pty Ltd,
15–25 Helles Avenue, Moorebank, NSW 2170,
and in New Zealand by Transworld Publishers (NZ) Ltd,
3 William Pickering Drive, Albany, Auckland.

Printed and bound in Great Britain by
Cox & Wyman Ltd, Reading, Berkshire.

To Michael Ari Groopman

Chapter 1

The gym at Sweet Valley High was stuffy, with a faint odor of sweat socks. Elizabeth Wakefield felt hot and sticky from dancing. But when the disc jockey announced a Beach Boys tune, her boyfriend grabbed her hand and yanked her back onto the dance floor.

"Todd!" Elizabeth cried, laughing at his eagerness. "I'm thirsty!"

"But it's 'California Girls'!" Todd Wilkins protested over the sound of the electronic organ. "We can't *not* dance to this tune!"

"We'll dance to the next one," Elizabeth promised. "I need a soda right now."

"They wrote this song about *you*, Liz," Todd said. "You have an obligation!"

1

"Todd, this is southern California," she reminded him. "Every female in this room is a California girl!"

"But nobody looks the part the way you do!" he said, squeezing her hands.

"Except my sister," Elizabeth said, but she gave up and relaxed into the step. She loved dancing with Todd, to any music.

Todd rolled his eyes at the reference to Elizabeth's identical twin sister, Jessica. Elizabeth ignored his reaction. About the only thing Todd and Jessica had in common was that they were two of Elizabeth's favorite people. Elizabeth twirled under his outstretched arm and nearly bumped into another girl being similarly whirled. For a split second she thought she'd come close to colliding with her reflection in a mirror. But it was only Jessica, who seemed to have appeared by magic as soon as Elizabeth thought about her.

The sisters were used to being called the perfect California girls. With their blond hair, golden tans, and blue-green eyes the color of the Pacific Ocean, the description was inevitable.

Despite the twins' identical faces and size-six figures, their friends seldom mixed them up. Jessica's sun-streaked hair was exactly the same shade as her sister's, but unlike Elizabeth, who always arranged her hair in practical styles, Jessica wore hers in loose, sexy waves. For the dance that Saturday night Elizabeth's hair was pulled back in elegant pearl-encrusted barrettes; Jessica's flew out around her face as she danced, wild and free.

Elizabeth favored simple makeup—that night she wore only a touch of lip gloss and a hint of brown mascara. Her outfit for the informal dance—a floral-print dress a few inches above the knee—was flattering but not flashy. Jessica, on the other hand, had been turning heads all evening in her white spaghetti-strap minidress. Her eyes were dramatically lined with sultry shadow, and she wore a deep red lipstick.

"*I wish they all could be California girls!*" Jessica sang, gleefully off-key, as Danny Porter spun her under his upraised arm. "They're playing our song, Liz!" she called to her sister. "Isn't this awesome?"

"I thought you didn't like oldies, Jessica," Todd replied over the music. He watched Danny and Jessica for a moment and then maneuvered Elizabeth into a complicated "pretzel" sequence that left her dizzy.

"Well, I wouldn't be caught dead just *listening*

3

to the Beach Boys," Jessica called back, eyeing the other couple's dance moves. "I mean, the newer the better, right? But *dancing* is different." She nodded to Danny, and they launched into a series of turns even more complex than Elizabeth and Todd's.

Todd responded by spinning Elizabeth until she had to clutch his shoulder to keep from toppling over. She was too tired to dance anymore, she decided, Beach Boys or not.

"You have to admit it, Liz," Todd said a little breathlessly. "As much as I hate to vote with Psycho Twin, this stuff is terrific to dance to!"

Jessica narrowed her eyes at the "psycho twin" reference but didn't comment on it, turning away from Todd pointedly to address her sister. "The Beach Boys are way cool for dancing," she said. "Unlike that depressing so-called music the DJ was playing a few minutes ago!"

Jessica and Todd never agreed about much of anything, but it was clear they were both having a great time. Elizabeth sighed. She liked the Beach Boys. But the folk ballad her sister had hated was one of Elizabeth's favorite new songs, a heartfelt lament about the destruction of the rain forests.

"Look around you, Liz!" Jessica exclaimed, as

if to prove her point. "All the coolest kids are on the dance floor now. It's jock city!"

Elizabeth glanced around. Sure enough, almost every student who'd danced to the slow ballad now stood near the refreshments table or around the edges of the room. They'd been replaced on the dance floor by some of the most popular kids at Sweet Valley High, especially those from the athletic teams and cheerleading squad, as well as the cliques known as the snobs and the fashion queens.

Jessica was a cocaptain of the cheerleaders; Danny, whom she occasionally dated, was a quiet but cute wide receiver for the school football team. Nearby, Bruce Patman, one of the richest and—in Elizabeth's opinion—most stuck-up people at school, twirled his girlfriend, Pamela Robertson. Both were expert tennis players with conservative taste in just about everything.

Tall, blond quarterback Ken Matthews was dancing with Lila Fowler, Jessica's wealthy and stylish best friend. Elizabeth knew Ken wasn't interested in Lila. But she was glad to see him back in the center of Sweet Valley High's social scene. He finally seemed to have recovered from his painful breakup with Jessica a few months earlier.

Even Todd counted as a jock—after all, he was the star of the school basketball team. Elizabeth sighed. Her own extracurricular interests centered around Sweet Valley High's student newspaper, the *Oracle*. Suddenly she felt out of place on the dance floor. *That's silly*, she scolded herself. These kids were her friends. Nobody cared that she didn't play a varsity sport. She pushed away her doubts and concentrated on having a good time.

"I don't know about the 'coolest' kids, but this song sure has the athletic crowd dancing the night away," she said to Todd. "Is there a cosmic connection between being a school athlete and liking the Beach Boys?"

"Nothing cosmic about it," Todd said. "Actually it's part of the tryout for team sports. If you can't sing the lyrics to at least one Beach Boys tune, you're on the bench." His brown eyes twinkled in the sexy way that always made Elizabeth's insides melt. She forgot about the music and the other couples and leaned against him as if it were a slow dance, relishing the feel of his hard, muscular chest against her cheek and the woodsy smell of his aftershave.

"You're throwing us off rhythm!" Todd complained.

"I'm too tired to be bounced around like your basketball. Let's dance slow!" She snuggled against him.

"Well, when you put it that way."

Elizabeth idly watched as her sister and Danny prep-stepped away across the floor. Then Bryce Fisherman, another football player, tapped Danny on the shoulder and appropriated Jessica. Danny cast him a dark look before retreating to the sidelines. Jessica's grin widened. She always loved being cut in on, Elizabeth reflected—as long as the guy doing the cutting was tall and cute.

"Jessica seems to be enjoying herself," she said. "Being fought over by two football players is right up her alley!"

Todd rolled his eyes. "It's hard to believe you two are genetic replicas."

Despite their identical appearances, the twins were nothing alike when it came to guys. Jessica's motto was The More the Merrier. Dancing and partying were as natural to her as breathing and a lot more fun. As far as she was concerned, school was a place for socializing; classes were annoyances to be endured between lunch and cheerleading practice.

Elizabeth preferred to spend her time with one special boy, Todd—though her sister thought it was silly for a sixteen-year-old to be tied down. Elizabeth enjoyed parties and dances, but they were secondary to more serious pursuits, like studying hard so she could get into a top college and realize her dream of becoming a professional writer.

"Jessica may get her kicks from causing dissension on the football team," Elizabeth said. "But at the moment I don't have the energy to dance with one basketball player, even if he is the cutest guy in the room!"

The DJ put on another Beach Boys song, but Todd finally allowed her to pull him off the dance floor to grab a soda.

As the a cappella opening of "Barbara Ann" filled the school gym Jessica was psyched to see Danny tapping Bryce's shoulder to cut back in. She smiled and shrugged at Bryce to let him know she wanted to dance with him but didn't have any choice. She turned an even more dazzling smile on Danny. Both boys were definite hunks, and she liked them equally—as friends. Obviously they felt more strongly about her. As they vied for her attention Jessica knew she was exactly where she wanted to be. She got a tremendous rush from having cute guys fight over her.

The second Beach Boys song was another hit with the jocks on the dance floor. Left without a partner, Bryce jumped to the center of the gym and started playing air guitar. Two other football players, linebackers Michael Lewis and Tad Johnson, ran to join him, bouncing to the tune and singing into their fists. Their friends from the sports teams and cheerleading squad laughed and clapped.

Not everyone was so enthusiastic.

"Bubblegum pop!" jeered Jan Brown from the bleachers. The seats had been folded and pushed against the wall, but the tall, scowling girl had climbed to the top. Now she surveyed the gym from that vantage point, along with her usual crowd—a group of rough kids Jessica's friends called the burnouts.

"Put on something that won't give us diabetes!" pleaded Justin Belson. The auburn-haired junior wasn't as obnoxious as his friends, Jessica thought. But he had zero taste in music. She'd heard his boom box blasting heavy metal from the loading ramp behind the cafeteria as he and his friends sneaked a cigarette at lunchtime.

"We need some metal, man. Heavy metal rules!" called out Nicky Shepard from the other end of the top bleacher. He was blond and ruggedly handsome, but Jessica had decided long ago that he wasn't her type.

"Crawl back in your holes, freakazoids!" suggested Bruce.

Danny maneuvered Jessica closer to the DJ's table, where Elizabeth and Todd were now standing with a group of hippies, artistic types, and other kids Jessica thought of as total flakes. For a moment she wondered why her twin's friend Enid Rollins wasn't there, playing what Jessica thought of as her usual role as Elizabeth's loyal but boring sidekick. Then she remembered Enid was at Lake Tahoe for the weekend, visiting her aunt.

Jessica overheard somebody asking the DJ, "How about some rap?" Jessica hated rap music. She and Danny danced slower so they could listen in on the conversation.

"Rap's cool, but after that I vote for some punk," suggested Dana Larson. Dana was lead singer for Sweet Valley High's punk-rock band, the Droids, and everyone thought of her as head of the punk contingent at school. "Have you guys heard Nose Ring's new tune?"

Jessica wrinkled her nose. *Nose Ring?* she mouthed to Danny. He raised one eyebrow as the DJ started thumbing through her collection for rap and punk.

"I've heard it," Maria Slater said. "It's totally solid!" The tall, striking African American girl was one of Elizabeth's closest friends. She'd lived in New York City and had been a child actress in Hollywood. She was more sophisticated than most kids in town. Maria wasn't exactly a punker; Jessica thought of her as more of a brainiac, like Enid, despite Maria's exciting past. *Whatever,* Jessica thought dismissively. Maria was obviously as clueless about music as most of the hippies, artists, and brains who clustered around Elizabeth.

"Got any Colleen Dunstan?" asked Olivia Davidson, a poet and painter who was a friend of Elizabeth's and the arts editor for the *Oracle*.

Jessica and Danny rolled their eyes at each other. Olivia's request was no surprise. Dunstan's brand of alternative rock was totally undanceable, but Jessica figured that wouldn't matter to Olivia. She hadn't seen the curly-haired junior dance once all night. In fact, she knew it had been weeks since Olivia even had a date—not since she'd broken up with her art-student boyfriend, Harry Minton.

"Great idea, Olivia!" Elizabeth said. "I love Dunstan's new album."

Jessica and Danny abandoned dancing so they could prevent a musical disaster. Luckily

11

Todd was already there coming to the rescue.

"Colleen Dunstan?" Todd exclaimed with a grimace. "No way! Nobody can dance to that female complaint rock!"

Elizabeth's eyebrows went up. "I *like* Colleen Dunstan!"

Todd shrugged. "Her voice is OK. But who wants to hear somebody moaning about people fighting in Ireland? What we need around here are party tunes!"

"What's wrong with meaningful lyrics?" Elizabeth demanded.

"If I want to learn about civil wars, I'll go to history class," Jessica put in.

"Jess is right, Liz," Todd said. He winced as he realized what he'd said. "We're not at school now—well, at least we're not in class."

"I must have missed the table where we were required to check our brains at the door," Maria said.

"I don't want to have to *think* about the music," Todd protested. He turned to Elizabeth with what Jessica thought of as his puppy dog look. "I just want to have fun with my favorite California girl."

"Excuse me while I throw up," Jessica said.

"The Beach Boys are fun," Elizabeth said.

"But honestly, Todd, 'Ba-Ba-Ba-Ba-Barbara Ann'? You've got to admit—the lyrics are way shallow!"

"Lighten up! We're here to have fun," Todd reminded her.

Jessica watched the argument as if it were a tennis match. She'd always said Elizabeth and Todd were in a rut. A good, rousing disagreement might be just the ticket to add some spice to their boring, steady relationship.

Olivia Davidson was beginning to wonder why she'd bothered coming to the dance. She hated the Beach Boys. And her classmates' good-natured squabbling was getting on her nerves. Even her dress was wrong. Its loose, flowing layers of violet and indigo were hand-painted with abstract forms in delicate gold lines. The dress had captivated her at a Los Angeles shop that specialized in merchandise handmade by women in underdeveloped countries. But compared to the mall-store outfits of the other teens, she felt downright weird.

Olivia was used to being considered different. Lately, though, she'd felt lonely. Losing Harry had been difficult, but now she felt ready to start dating again. Unfortunately none of the guys she knew was interested. She had to admit that few of them held any interest for her either.

The music changed to a driving rap beat. Olivia was relieved. She didn't think much of the music itself; it sounded pretty tuneless to her. But at least the lyrics were trying to say something. Besides, it was fun to watch the jocks on the dance floor stare around them in dismay.

"What's with the urban commando crap?" Bryce yelled.

"This stuff sucks!" bellowed Jan from her perch atop the bleachers. For once, Olivia noted, the burnouts and the jocks agreed about something.

"Beach Boys! Beach Boys! Beach Boys!" chanted Tad. He seemed to throw his entire 240-pound bulk into the effort, and his deep voice rang out over the gym. *It's easy to see why his nickname is "Blubber,"* Olivia thought. He was easily the biggest guy in the room. Some of the other football players joined in Tad's chant, including his younger brother, Zack, a sophomore who also played defense.

"Rap reeks!" Bruce Patman yelled out after the football team's chant dissolved into the general din. "Somebody put that CD player out of its misery!"

Lila Fowler left her dance partner and flounced over to the DJ's table, where Olivia and the others were still standing. "If Bruce Patman were any stupider, we'd have to water him twice a week," Lila observed. "But in this case he's right. Rap is totally fatal."

"No argument here," said Todd. "I don't have a clue about how to dance to this."

"It's not my first choice," Dana said, "but at least it's new and exciting!"

"If you want new and exciting, let's have the DJ put on something from Jamie Peters's latest CD," Jessica suggested.

"No way!" Keith Wagner objected. "Jamie Peters is mega-mainstream!" Olivia didn't know Keith very well. The closest thing Sweet Valley High had to an East Village poet and musician, he had dated Jessica briefly. He was cute, with thick, dark brown hair. But his back-to-nature wardrobe and his environmental activism had quickly convinced Jessica that he was too weird. These days Keith seemed to be more interested in self-expression than in saving the whales, but Olivia knew that wouldn't go over any better with a girl like Jessica.

Olivia suppressed a sigh. Between them, Jessica and Lila had dated every good-looking boy at school. *And I can't even get one to dance with me!*

"Jamie Peters is a *god*," Jessica corrected Keith.

"I wouldn't go that far, but he sure beats this sucky stuff," Todd said. "At least we can *dance* to Jamie Peters!"

"It's not hard to dance to rap," Dana said. "It's got a great beat." The tall blond girl shuffled onto the dance floor alone, her hips swaying in tight black leggings with a studded, low-slung belt. Olivia thought she looked sexy and confident as she moved with the beat. From the expressions on the faces of the guys near the DJ stand, it was clear that they thought so too.

"Right," Olivia said to Elizabeth in a low voice, staring enviously at Dana's slim, graceful figure in a skintight midriff top with a vintage lace bra on the outside. Dana knew exactly who she was and where she fit in. "I would look about as idiotic trying to dance like Dana as I'd look wearing her outfit!"

"Me too!" Elizabeth agreed with a chuckle. "Same with her nose ring. But it works for Dana!"

That's the difference between me and

16

Elizabeth, Olivia thought. *She can laugh because she knows she fits in somewhere. She doesn't have to feel insecure around girls like Dana.*

"Are you OK?" Elizabeth asked in a whisper.

Olivia forced a smile. "I'm fine," she said. "It's just so hot in here."

An hour later Elizabeth could feel the tension in the air, as oppressive as the heat. Elizabeth and Todd had retired to one end of the gym, where the music wasn't quite as loud. There they found seats at a crowded table where they could watch the action without being drawn in.

The DJ was doing her best to alternate the music and keep everyone happy, but the factions of students were becoming more vocal about their preferences. A heavy-metal anthem was blasting away, its driving bass line drowning out the complaints of Bruce, Tad, and some of the other jocks who were now clustered around the refreshments table. Jan still presided like a surly queen from her throne atop the bleachers, but Justin and some of the other burnouts were swaying back and forth on the dance floor, hardly lifting their feet.

"They call that dancing?" Todd exclaimed.

17

Elizabeth shrugged. "If it makes them happy, why not?"

"Those dudes are just hanging out, feeling the beat," Keith explained.

"Those 'dudes' look like they haven't showered in a week," Lila replied, wrinkling her nose.

"It's called the grunge look," Maria Slater explained.

"*Grunge* is a good word for it," Lila said, eyeing the dancers with disdain. "During evolution their ancestors must have been in the control group."

"Thank goodness this so-called song is ending," Todd said.

"Play something we can dance to!" Tad yelled over the last chorus. From across the room Elizabeth watched as he slammed his paper cup of soda down on the refreshments table, spilling its contents. Then he was striding toward the disc jockey, his hands gesturing dramatically.

Bryce left Jessica's side and hurried after his teammate, apparently trying to reason with the enraged linebacker. Even on the verge of a crisis, Elizabeth noticed, Jessica automatically sidled up to Danny as soon as she found herself alone. But Tad threw off Bryce's hands like a quarterback resisting a tackle.

18

"No more freak music!" Tad bellowed at the disc jockey.

"Who are you calling 'freaks'?" Jan screamed down from the bleachers.

Tad cursed up at her, the disc jockey temporarily forgotten. By now heads were turning all over the gym.

"What's with Tad?" Todd asked Ken.

"Why pick on Tad?" Lila objected. "Jan isn't exactly Miss Congeniality."

"But Jan's always like that," Todd said. "I've never seen Blubber acting so loud and obnoxious!"

"He's a linebacker," Maria said, as if it explained everything.

Ken shook his head. "I don't know what's up. The Blub has been a wild man all week! Yesterday at practice he rammed Danny too hard, and Coach Schultz had to bench him for the rest of the afternoon."

"I think something's bothering Tad lately," Todd said. "What's his brother have to say about it?"

"Zack isn't talking either," Ken replied.

Roger Collins, a teacher who was acting as a dance chaperon, materialized at Tad's side. He pulled the boy aside and appeared to be lecturing him, the teacher's handsome features calm but stern. Elizabeth couldn't hear what the *Oracle*'s faculty sponsor was saying, but she guessed from his gestures that he was warning Tad to calm down or leave the dance.

"Mr. Collins will handle it," Elizabeth said, relieved. "He always does." Her favorite teacher had a firm-but-fair demeanor that usually convinced even the most riled-up students to control their tempers.

A guitar riff announced the next song, a cut from the new Jamie Peters CD that Jessica had been raving about.

"Excellent!" Bruce Patman declared. A cheer went up from the crowd around the refreshments table, and Elizabeth relaxed a little. At least Tad's overcast face was beginning to clear. He grabbed Claire Middleton's hand and led her away from her date and onto the dance floor. Tall, dark-haired Claire, second-string quarterback for the team, was the first girl in the district to play varsity football.

"This music is more like it!" Todd said, making a thumbs-up sign.

Keith shook his head. "Not even!" he complained. "I may hurl if I hear one more Jamie Peters song."

Todd ignored him. "Come on, Liz! Let's dance!"

"I'm all danced out," Elizabeth said. She wasn't tired so much as fed up. Some of the kids were taking this little music war way too seriously. The look on Tad's face a few minutes earlier had made her nervous.

"How about you, Maria?" Todd asked. "Are you up for a dance?"

Maria ran a hand over her short-cropped black hair. "No, thanks. No offense, but Jamie Peters is too middle-of-the-road for me. I like music with more of an edge—"

"How can anyone not like Jamie Peters?" Lila demanded.

"This music is for nimrods!" Nicky yelled as if he'd heard her comment from across the dance floor.

Most of the heavy-metal fans had cleared out when they heard the opening riff of the pop song. But Justin stood in the center of the room, his arms crossed. The athletes on the dance floor stepped around him as if he were a tree.

Bryce cast a rueful glance at Jessica, who was dancing once again with Danny. He sighed and pulled Lila onto the dance floor instead.

Keith nodded toward Lila and Bryce. "I al-

21

ways thought Lila the Ice Princess was more of a fashion queen than a jockette," he said.

"She is," Maria said. "But fashion queens and jocks have one thing in common—a lack of imagination about music! I mean—"

"Uh-oh," Keith said, interrupting her. "Here comes trouble—with a capital T that rhymes with B, and that stands for Blubber."

Elizabeth followed his gaze.

Justin still stood in the center of the dance floor. Tad "Blubber" Johnson danced close to him, his arms around Claire but his eyes on the skinny, long-haired boy. Tad stepped to the side suddenly, brushing roughly against Justin's arm. Justin stumbled, swearing, but righted himself and stood his ground, staring up at the line-backer, who outweighed him by more than a hundred pounds.

"You're in my way, loser!" Tad yelled.

"I'm not moving until we hear some music that's worth moving to," Justin said, his voice high-pitched and boyish after Tad's deep rumbles. He called to the disc jockey, "Do you have anything by Loaded Chain Saw?"

Elizabeth glanced around the room for Mr. Collins. He was at the side entrance, pushing a group of burnouts into the gym, probably after catching them smoking outside the door. The English teacher hadn't yet noticed the standoff in the center of the room, and he was too far away for Elizabeth to alert him.

"Make that some classic Motown!" Tad called toward the DJ's table. Nobody was dancing now.

"You jocks think you're so tough, but you listen to wuss music!" Justin replied. His voice carried across the room. Mr. Collins looked up, a worried expression on his face, and started pushing through the students who had gathered at the edge of the dance floor. Elizabeth saw Tad's brother, Zack, also pushing his way toward the center of the room.

Tad grabbed the collar of Justin's oversize, faded flannel shirt. "If you know what's good for you, you'll take that back, dirtball!"

"That's telling him, Blubber!" Bruce Patman called from a safe distance.

Justin had eyes for no one but Tad.

"What are you going to do, you dumb jock? Tackle him?" Jan jeered from her spot on top of the bleachers. Neither Justin nor Tad turned at the sound of her voice.

Claire stood on tiptoes to say something into Tad's ear, but he shrugged her away. He glared down at Justin and shook his head in disgust. For a moment Elizabeth thought the linebacker would turn on his heel and stomp away across the dance floor. Tad was big, but she'd never known him to be violent—except, perhaps, on the football field.

Then he drew back one beefy fist and landed a punch squarely in the smaller boy's midsection.

Claire screamed as Justin crumpled to the glossy wooden floor. Elizabeth felt as if the wind had been knocked out of her. She clutched at her stomach and grabbed Todd's arm for support.

Mr. Collins, still too far away to stop the fight, began yelling, but Elizabeth couldn't make out the teacher's words over the roar of voices that suddenly swelled to fill the room.

Justin grabbed for Tad's leg and managed to pull him to the floor. Tad kicked him savagely, and Justin reached for his own left arm, as if in pain. Bruce leaped forward to join in the fray, but Claire grabbed his elbow and jerked him out of the way.

"Thank goodness for Claire!" Elizabeth breathed to Todd. "If Bruce joined in the fight, every jock on the dance floor would be on top of Justin within seconds."

Only a minute had passed since Tad threw

the first punch, but it seemed like an hour before Mr. Collins reached the boys and pulled Tad to his feet. Coach Schultz stomped up right behind the English teacher, and Zack reached his brother at the same time. The coach gave Tad a hard glare and then knelt beside Justin. The disc jockey turned off the music, and the room was utterly silent as the coach helped the injured boy to his feet.

"This dance is over!" Mr. Collins announced in a loud, firm voice, still holding Tad by the shoulder. "All students are to leave the school immediately, in a quiet and orderly manner."

Coach Schultz pointed to Tad. "Except you."

Chapter 2

Olivia tossed the hand-painted violet-and-indigo dress onto her bed and pulled on her tie-dyed pajamas. Then she flicked on her computer and settled herself into her desk chair. It was too bad that the dance had ended in violence, she thought. But the truth was that she didn't mind having to go home early. She'd spent most of the evening standing on the sidelines, feeling lonely and uncomfortable as she watched her class-mates divide up into cliques.

As the operating system's main screen blos-somed onto the monitor with a musical chime, Olivia curled her bare toes around the legs of her chair and leaned forward in anticipation. She reached for her trackball and clicked on the icon for Virtual Hangout, an on-line service especially for teenagers.

She grinned as she navigated her way to the southern California chat room. On-line, she felt comfortable and free. She was always one of the gang, even if she didn't belong to any particular clique at school. Nobody in cyberspace cared that her unruly hair was frizzing wildly around her face or that the room around her was cluttered with paintbrushes, books, and papers. It didn't matter that she had just spent two hours at a school dance without having a single guy ask her onto the dance floor. She could just be herself and have people judge her by what she said and how she thought, not by what she wore or who her friends were.

Her computer screen told her she was now in her favorite chat room. Seconds later one of the other regulars greeted her, the words appearing on her screen like magic.

"Hey, Freeverse!" ChitCat said, calling Olivia by her screen name.

Olivia had never thought to ask if ChitCat was a boy or a girl; it had always seemed irrelevant. Everyone used a screen name in VHO, and people were more interested in hearing what she had to say than in fitting her into a category.

"Haven't heard from you in a few days, FV," said another on-line acquaintance, a boy who called himself JohnnyB. *"What's shaking?"*

"Hi, all!" Olivia typed. *"Anyone ever feel all alone in a room full of people? :("* She ended with an emoticon, a frowning face that could be read sideways, and then hit enter to send the message.

"You know it!" ChitCat replied. *"But never in this room!"*

Olivia nodded to herself. ChitCat was absolutely right.

"Excellent!" Danny Porter announced. "You can't beat good, old-fashioned California beach music."

Ken Matthews cranked up the volume on the stereo in his family's living room, where the athletic crowd had decided to continue the party.

"I'd like to beat some of those hippies and burnouts who wrecked the dance for all of us!" Bruce Patman said.

Ken didn't believe in violence, but he knew Bruce was mostly talk. Besides, Justin and his friends had said some harsh things about student athletes back at the dance.

"Can you believe those creepy, freaked-out

losers?" Jessica asked, leaning casually on Bryce Fisherman's shoulder. "We're the ones who are important to the school! Especially big, strong football players," she added, stroking Bryce's cheek with one finger. "Justin Belson's biggest contribution to Sweet Valley High is a cloud of clove cigarette smoke!"

Watching Jessica alternate her flirting between Bryce and Danny all night, Ken had felt twinges of an emotion he couldn't quite define. It wasn't jealousy. She'd burned him badly, but Ken could finally say he was over Jessica Wakefield. Still, it bothered him to see her hanging all over his teammates. After a quick glance around the room, he realized it wasn't just Jessica who was making him feel hollow inside. It was totally depressing, watching all the happy couples.

Bruce had his arms around Pamela. Amy Sutton, a cheerleader Ken had dated earlier in the year, was giving her tennis-player boyfriend, Barry Rork, a peck on the cheek. Claire, Ken's second-string backup at quarterback, was wiping a spot of onion dip from her teammate Michael Lewis's collar. Claire had been dating the powerful linebacker since a few weeks after he'd transferred to Sweet Valley High—since just after

Jessica refused to go steady with Michael.

Ken sighed, noticing the way the new line-backer was now staring not at Jessica but at Claire. Michael had found somebody to take Jessica's place, but Ken was still alone.

Ken had gone out with a few girls after he and Jessica had broken up, but now he wanted more than a fling. He wanted a romance. He hadn't realized how much he missed having a steady relationship.

He reminded himself that plenty of people didn't have dates. Even Lila had come alone that night, and it didn't seem to bother her. He watched speculatively as she cast her discerning brown eyes over his hastily arranged spread of potato chips and nachos. Lila was known for hosting the hottest parties in town and was no doubt unimpressed with what he'd thrown together on the spur of the moment.

Lila was pretty, Ken thought. She was slender and graceful, with light brown hair that always gleamed. He'd danced with her a few times that night—they'd even gone out now and then. She was a bit of a snob, but she was popular and fun, the kind of girl Ken knew he should want to date. Heck, everyone wanted to date Lila. She was one of his crowd. She fit in with these people the same way Ken did. So why didn't he feel a single spark of romance when he looked at her?

Of course, he'd felt enough sparks with Jessica for an entire forest fire. Jessica was also the "right" kind of girl for Ken. She was bubbly and sexy. She loved sports; she had more school spirit than the pep club and the marching band combined. And she was always ready to party. *But look how that relationship turned out*, Ken reminded himself.

Unfortunately there wasn't a girl in the room who attracted him the way Jessica used to.

"What makes me postal isn't the burnouts," Danny was saying as Ken wrenched his attention back to the conversation. "It's the hippies and the artsy-fartsy types. Man, those kids are weird city!"

"I know what you mean," Barry agreed. "Have you ever tried to have a discussion with Keith Wagner?"

Lila laughed. "Jessica actually went out with him a few times!"

Bryce and Danny both stared at Jessica, eyebrows raised. Jessica cast Lila a dark glare. "That wasn't me!" she insisted. "My body was possessed by space aliens at the time."

"Well, Keith's definitely from another planet,"

Amy said. "Do you know he won't even wear leather shoes? He's always in those clunky back-to-nature sandals. He says they're 'cruelty-free.' He doesn't eat meat either."

"Maybe I should ask him out for prime rib some night," Lila said dryly. "I'll wear my fur-lined parka."

"Then there's Ted Jenson, Mr. Dramatic Poetry Readings," Jessica added, rolling her eyes. "I can't believe Maria sometimes goes out with that flake!"

Winston Egbert, widely known as the junior-class clown, turned to his girlfriend in mock surprise. "Is there something you're not telling me?"

Maria Santelli shook her head. "Not me, silly. The other Maria. You know, Maria Slater."

"Elizabeth's friend. The *other* Wakefield," Bruce said with an accusatory glance at Jessica. "The twin who dragged Whizzer Wilkins out to the Dairi Burger tonight with the flake contingent instead of letting him come here with his fellow jocks, where he belongs! That's what Todd gets for dating out of his class!"

"Watch it, Patman!" Jessica said coldly. She often made fun of Elizabeth herself, but she could be downright vicious when somebody else attacked her twin.

"I don't care what the flakes and the burnouts wear or who they go out with," Ken said, steering the conversation away from the subject of Elizabeth. "But it irks me when they call us 'dumb jocks.' I mean, who are they to say something like that? We're the real heart of the school!"

Winston put his hands on his hips. "I thought *I* was the heart of the school!"

"You're certainly not its brain," Lila reflected.

"OK, then I'll be the gallbladder," Winston decided, nodding. "Yes, definitely the gallbladder."

"I've always said you had a lot of gall," Maria put in.

"Justin Belson had a lot of gall," Claire said, "to go up against two-hundred-and-forty pounds of Blubber, as scrawny as he is! And Justin calls us athletes dumb?"

"Justin is projecting," Amy explained in her hot-line-volunteer voice. "He deals with his own insecurities by transferring them onto everyone else. When he says 'dumb jock,' subconsciously he's afraid that—"

"He's afraid that Amy will bore everyone to tears with her Project Youth psychobabble," Jessica concluded.

Amy turned on her. "You are such a brat!"

"So what'll happen to Tad?" Michael asked. "Obviously Collins and the coach think he's responsible for the fight."

"Blubber will have so much detention, his grandchildren will be staying after school," Winston predicted.

"That is so unfair!" Amy complained. "The fight was Justin's fault and Jan's. They provoked him."

"True," Lila said. "But Tad has been wigged out lately. He really did lose it."

"They both lost it," Jessica said. "It's hard to blame Blubber. Justin left him no choice. But I still hate it when guys try to settle things by punching each other out."

"I say he had every right to punch out that little weenie," Amy said staunchly. "Justin got what he deserved!"

Ken tuned out the conversation. Like most of the girls in their crowd—most of the girls he'd ever dated—Amy was gorgeous and athletic. But all those relationships had ended badly. *Why?* he asked himself. For the first time he wondered if it was a good idea to spend so much time with the same group of people. Maybe he should broaden his horizons by asking out a girl who was totally different—who was into rap music, Zen, or body piercing. He chuckled to himself, imagining Bruce's reaction.

Todd wasn't the only athlete who'd ever dated outside the clique. Right there, in Ken's own living room, cheerleader Maria Santelli was gazing adoringly at Winston Egbert. The only nonjock present, Winston was so klutzy he could hardly walk without tripping over his big feet— let alone play a team sport. But his wacky sense of humor made him welcome in any crowd. Winston and Maria were a fixture at Sweet Valley High jock parties.

I dated Elizabeth myself, Ken thought, *even if nobody knew about it!* Early that year Todd's family had moved east for a few months—and Ken had begun dating Elizabeth secretly. They'd broken it off as soon as Todd came back to Sweet Valley. And later Ken decided Jessica was the twin for him—the twin who shared his interests and outlook. Now he wondered how important those similarities really were.

"I haven't been at this school for long, but what Ken said before was right on." Michael spoke up in his soft southern accent. The mention of his own name pulled Ken's attention back to the conversation. "It's easy to see that it's the

35

jocks who are at the center of school life. Not the burnouts, the hippies, or the punkers."

"True," Ken said, though part of his mind was still wondering if the "right" kind of girl could be all wrong for him. "Look at the things that bring the entire student body together!"

"Things like dissing the cafeteria food?" Claire asked, her eyes twinkling.

Ken smiled. "You know what I mean. The whole social scene revolves around sports and teams! Football games, basketball games—"

"Tennis matches," Bruce and Pamela said in unison, before looking at each other and bursting into laughter.

"Soccer games, swim meets, softball—" Maria said.

"And pep rallies, and victory parties, and cheerleading competitions," Jessica added.

Amy jumped onto the coffee table, waving imaginary pom-poms. *"Gimme a* J! *Gimme an* O! *Gimme a* C *and a* K!"

"Let's hear it for the jocks, hoo-rah-ray!" Jessica concluded in her best cheerleading voice.

Everyone began laughing, and somebody turned up the stereo—the Beach Boys again— for some dancing. But Amy's voice carried above the clamor.

"Jocks rule supreme!" she declared. "We don't need anybody else!"

Ken laughed and cheered along with the crowd. But secretly he wasn't so sure that this was all he needed.

Chapter 3

Usually the twins rode to school together, but on Monday morning Jessica was alone in the Jeep. Elizabeth had caught a ride with Olivia to make an early newspaper staff meeting. Without her more organized twin to keep her punctual, Jessica arrived too late to find a space in the front parking lot, though she still had plenty of time before homeroom. She steered around to the back of the school to snag a space.

As she walked past the loading ramp on her way to the main entrance Jessica coughed at the pall of smoke that always hung over the place.

"Yo, Wakefield!" called Keith Wagner. He was sharing a clove cigarette with Justin, whose left arm was in a sling.

"Oh, great. It's Thing One and Thing Two," Jessica said.

"I saw the best arms of my generation maimed by jocks," Keith announced in a tone of voice that reminded Jessica of somebody reciting poetry. Very bad poetry.

"I haven't the faintest idea what you're talking about," Jessica said. "Let's keep it that way." She couldn't remember why she'd ever thought Keith was cute. Today he wore a pair of ragged, fringed jeans under an embroidered gauze shirt that Jessica thought might have been in style when her parents were in high school. His dark hair was thick and long, but she wondered when it had last seen a bottle of shampoo.

"What I'm talking about is might ain't right," Keith said, his voice growing louder.

"You made a rhyme!" Jessica exclaimed. "Your parents must be so proud."

Keith blew a mouthful of clove-scented smoke at her and handed the cigarette to Justin, who was leaning against the smoke-stained stucco wall, watching them with a blank expression on his face.

"You jocks just had to run the show Saturday night," Keith said accusingly. "You couldn't be mellow and let the rest of the dudes hang loose."

39

Jessica crossed her arms in front of her. "Do you come with subtitles?"

Keith pointed at Justin's sling. "What I'm saying is, look what you and your fascist friends did to yon innocent youth!"

With his good arm Justin reached under his grungy flannel shirt. He pulled a fist-size beanbag ball from the pocket of a pair of black jeans that were at least three sizes too big for him and began absently turning the ball in his hand, staring at it as if it might speak.

Jessica shrugged. "He always acts like he's been lobotomized. All of your crowd does."

"I'm talking about the arm, man! You bruised the dude's arm, sprained his wrist."

"I get it," Jessica said. "Justin and Tad tried to bash in each other's pointy little rock-filled heads. And that's my fault just because I happened to dance with two football players that night."

Keith held his hands out from his sides. "If you're not with us, you're against us."

"Another insightful analysis from the mind of the boy poet," Jessica said.

Justin slid his back down the wall until he was sitting on the concrete ramp. Then he blew a series of clove-scented smoke rings that hung in the air between Jessica and Keith.

"I know you, Jessica," Keith said, his voice suddenly intense. "You pretend to be one of the cleat clique, but you're not really like them."

"No? What am I really like?"

"You have too much love inside you to hang with those thugs," Keith protested. "But you're denying the positive vibes. You just go on shaking your pom-poms and urging those pumped-up Ken dolls to smash each other."

"Normal people call it cheerleading," Jessica replied.

"You should be wearing flowers in your hair and spreading love and peace!"

Jessica rolled her eyes. "Excuse me while I kiss the sky," she said, reciting a line from a Jimi Hendrix song she'd heard a few times. "That is so thirty years ago."

"Jocks are pigs in any decade."

"*They're* pigs?" Jessica yelled, outraged. "And this from a guy wearing hand-me-down jeans that haven't been washed since Woodstock?"

"How can you dig having those jerks from the football team follow you around like a line of baby geese?" Keith asked.

"Those are my friends you're talking about!"

"Football players are nobody's friends," Keith insisted. "They're Neanderthals with overdeveloped biceps and padding for brains."

"What happened to all that 'love your neighbor' stuff you're always spouting?" Jessica challenged.

"The neighborhood went downhill," Keith said. "I can't believe you actually like those animals! Take the Blubbermeister. If you ask me, the dude has rammed his head into a few too many opposing pectorals."

"Blubber's a perfectly nice guy!" Jessica objected. "He's just been upset this week, that's all."

"Face it, Jess. Some of us drink from the fountain of knowledge. Blubber gargled."

"That's it!" Jessica cried. "I don't have to stand here and listen to—"

"Chill, dudes," Justin interrupted in a quiet but commanding voice. He exhaled a long, slow stream of clove smoke. "You two should learn to be laid-back."

"Yeah, and spend my days playing zombie on the ramp with the rest of you vegetables!" Jessica retorted.

That is it, she told herself as she stormed away. At first she'd thought Tad was out of line, using Justin as a punching bag at the dance. Now she decided he'd been totally justified. She just wished he'd socked Keith too—right in his smug little hippie face.

Ken's blue eyes scanned the list of professional hockey scores on his computer screen Tuesday morning. He didn't know how he ever managed to keep up with sports before his parents bought him a computer. Somewhere on-line he could find the latest news on everything from scrimmages to play-offs, from baseball to wrestling, from high school to the pros.

"Get a move on, Ken!" came his father's voice from the hallway. "You don't want to be late for school!"

"That's debatable," Ken muttered under his breath. If the tension at school was anything like the day before, in the wake of Justin and Tad's fight over the weekend, well, he'd be much happier sitting in his bedroom all day, surfing the Internet. But he couldn't exactly say that to his father. "I'll be outta here in a minute," he said instead, "as soon as I finish up."

He had one more item to check on, and it was a crucial one. Nearby El Carro High School had played top-ranked Compton in football the night before. His own Sweet Valley Gladiators were up against the El Carro Cougars on Friday, so he had to know how the Compton game turned out.

He punched in the address of El Carro's Web site and navigated to the sports page.

"Cougars win, twenty-one to twenty," he read aloud. "What a major coup! I wonder how they pulled it off." He scrolled down, searching for a full article, but there was nothing but a final score for the Compton game and an impassioned plea about Friday's game, beginning *"Crush Sweet Valley . . ."*

"No stats? No play-by-play?" he complained. "This Web page is a joke!" He'd have to find the information some other way. He glanced at the clock radio on his nightstand. If he skipped breakfast, he could stay in cyberspace another ten minutes and still make it to school on time.

Maybe somebody on-line can tell me, Ken thought. He navigated to Virtual Hangout and clicked on the southern California chat room. Few high-school students would be on-line at this time of day. But all he needed was one El Carro football fan who could give him the scoop on the team's new quarterback.

"Anyone from El Carro here?" he typed in, using his screen name, Quarter.

"A quarter of what?" somebody named Freeverse replied.

Ken sighed. He had to admit that lately he'd

been feeling about a quarter fulfilled. He shrugged and typed that in. It was a dorky thought, but that was the beauty of being on-line. He could be as dorky as the chess club, and nobody would know it was him. Besides, he was spying for the enemy team. He couldn't exactly tell this El Carro student that "Quarter" was short for quarterback. As in Sweet Valley High's quarterback. As in the quarterback who would lead the drive to crush the Cougars come Friday night.

"A quarter fulfilled isn't half bad," replied Freeverse. *"That leaves plenty of space to fill with new experiences."*

Ken smiled. New experiences were just what he'd been craving. *"What kind of experiences?"* he asked, curious.

"Walking the road less traveled, fording the river uncrossed," Freeverse replied cryptically.

"Do you do those things?" he asked.

"I'd like to," said Freeverse.

"What else would you like to do?"

"Oh, I don't know. Paint scenes I've only imagined. Feel skirts of exotic silks swishing against my legs. Savor the taste of unpronounceable foods from distant places."

"To boldly go where no one has gone before, :)" Ken added, giving the emoticon for a smiling

45

face. *"You sound like an adventurer."* A female adventurer, he realized, thinking of the "swishing skirts" remark.

"An adventurer only in my dreams," said Freeverse. *"Sigh . . . :(In real life the biggest adventure I usually get is a walk along the beach, watching the gulls soar."*

His on-line friend had a way with words, Ken thought. *"You should write poetry."*

"I do," Freeverse admitted. *"Or I try to."*

"I bet it's awesome," he said. *"English is my worst subject. You sound like you'd be great at it."*

"I love to write."

Ken smiled ruefully, remembering a time he'd nearly flunked English and almost been kicked off the football team for it. *"Not me, Free,"* he admitted. *"But I do love walking on the beach. I'm nuts about seagulls too."*

"You ever wonder where they fly to?"

Ken started at the odd question, then shook his head. Abruptly he remembered that his correspondent couldn't see him. *"I guess I never thought about it,"* he keyed in. *"But wherever it is, I wish I could go there too. Somewhere where I could meet new people and . . ."* He grinned. *"Savor the taste of unpronounceable foods! :)"*

Freeverse was the most intriguing girl he'd "met" in a long time. She had beautiful thoughts and used beautiful words, and she was nothing at all like Jessica or Amy or any of the other girls who were part of his usual jock crowd. He suddenly wanted to get to know her better. As soon as he thought it she seemed to read his mind.

"I've revealed that I like to write and paint and walk on the beach," she said. *"But I still don't know anything about you. What are you like? What do you like? Besides seagulls, I mean."*

He began to type, *"I'm the quarterback for my school's football team, and I'm also into baseball, basketball—"* He stopped abruptly without hitting enter and drummed his fingers on the wrist rest in front of his keyboard. Did he really want to send this message? Freeverse had a sensitive nature—the soul of a poet. She'd probably think he was a dumb jock, just like those kids at the dance had said.

"Ken!" called his mother from downstairs, interrupting his thoughts. "Your homeroom starts in fifteen minutes!"

Ken backspaced to erase the message he'd begun. *"Oops,"* he said instead. *"The parental units are freaking out. I am soooo late for school!*

47

Sorry to cut this short, but I gotta book."

"Ouch!" replied Freeverse. *"I'm late too. Maybe we'll catch each other on-line later."*

"I hope so," Ken said aloud as he exited the chat room and turned off his computer. He wondered if Freeverse was a junior like him. He assumed she went to El Carro since she'd responded when he asked if there were any El Carro students in the chat room. Maybe he'd even seen her at a game sometime. He wondered if she was as beautiful as she sounded.

As he grabbed his books and pushed open the door he realized he hadn't learned anything about the El Carro football game. He shrugged. It just didn't seem as important as it had a few minutes ago. He would have to ask around at football practice. Maybe Claire or Danny had heard something.

Enid had arrived home from Lake Tahoe the night before. Now it was Tuesday morning, and Elizabeth was filling her in on the weekend's events as Enid drove her to school in Mrs. Rollins's blue hatchback. Jessica had taken the Jeep for an early morning cheerleading practice.

"I can't believe Tad actually hit him!" Enid

said, pushing her curly, reddish brown hair out of her eyes. "Tad's huge, but he always seemed like the 'gentle giant' type to me."

"The worst thing about it—I mean, besides Justin's sprained wrist—is the way people have been dividing into two camps since then," Elizabeth replied. "Justin's friends are vowing to get revenge on Tad."

"You said he got early morning detention every day before school for practically the rest of his life. Isn't that enough?"

"Some people say it's too much," Elizabeth said. "The jocks blame Justin and his group for Tad's punishment. Bruce Patman's egging the rest on, saying they need to get even."

"How do they plan to do that?" Enid asked, her green eyes wide. "Are they staging the battle of the jocks versus the burnouts?"

Elizabeth shook her head. "It's gone way past the jocks and burnouts," she said. "Everybody's involved now. The jocks have signed on the snobs and the student-politico types. The burnouts are bonding with punkers, artists, hippies, and brains."

"This is so bizarre," Enid said. "Everyone usually gets along just fine. I hate it when people take sides!" She pulled the car into a parking space.

Elizabeth bit her lip. "Me too. And I wouldn't even know which side to be on!"

"Me neither," Enid said. "I guess most kids would probably put me and Maria Slater in with the brains. But you're harder to categorize."

"I do hang out with a lot of different kinds of people," Elizabeth said.

"Your other two favorite sidekicks, Todd and Jess, are total jocks," Enid said as she climbed out of the hatchback.

"And I do a lot of special projects for Principal Cooper," Elizabeth said. "I've heard people call me a politico for that."

"You have punker friends like Dana. And artsy friends like DeeDee Gordon and Olivia— when she's not wearing her school-newspaper hat or her flower-child hat."

Elizabeth led the way toward the main entrance to the school. "That doesn't make it any easier to be at school this week, with World War Three busting out all over."

"It sounds like a good time to be Switzerland," Enid said. "Adopt a policy of complete neutrality."

"I wish I could," Elizabeth said. "But I can't help thinking Tad was a total bully, beating up on someone so much smaller and weaker."

50

Elizabeth pushed open the door and was surprised at the jumble of voices that swelled from the lobby, even louder than the usual morning din. "I wish we could find a way to prevent the war altogether," she said, distracted. More than a dozen students were gathered, jabbering excitedly, in front of a bulletin board that ordinarily contained nothing more unusual than notices of upcoming student council meetings. And the crowd was growing rapidly. Elizabeth heard some of the kids around the bulletin board hooting with laughter, but others spoke in angry tones.

Tall, slender Maria Slater was pushing her way out of the throng. "Maria, what is it?" Elizabeth asked.

Maria rolled her eyes. "An English test by none other than Tad Johnson, alias Blubber," she said. "Somebody posted it for all to see."

"Let me guess," Enid said. "The revenge of the burnouts?"

"It looks that way," Maria replied. "Personally I'm glad they got back at him. Tad is a disgrace. There's no excuse for picking a fight the way he did!"

"True, but test scores are supposed to be private!" Elizabeth objected. "Who posted it?"

51

Maria shrugged. "Round up the usual subjects. But I doubt anyone will take credit."

Elizabeth pushed her way into the crowd, and Maria and Enid followed. She looked up at the paper on the bulletin board. It was Tad's test on John Steinbeck, and at the top was a big, red letter grade printed in Mr. Collins's strong, angular hand.

"Oooh, a D-*plus!*" jeered Nicky Shepard, his pale blue eyes flashing. "Blubber's mama is going to be so proud!"

"What do you expect from a dumb jock?" Jan said with a laugh. "I bet Blubber kicks butt like that on all his schoolwork."

Bryce Fisherman shook his fist at her. "Someone else will be kicking some butt if you freaks keep getting in our faces!" Elizabeth held her breath. She'd never heard Bryce sound so angry.

"Is this the part where I'm supposed to be scared?" Jan asked.

"You might have to be," said Ted Jenson, part of the hippie-artist contingent. "Jocks aren't bright enough for any response except punching someone's face in!"

"And freaks aren't bright enough to show up for class, let alone take a test," Claire complained. "I've seen you all out there smoking on the ramp. Just because you don't care about your school or anything else—"

"That's bogus!" Jan said. "Why do I have to wear a football helmet—or a ditzy cheerleader uniform—to show I care about this school?"

Suddenly Elizabeth heard a familiar voice above the general rumbling. *"Ditzy?"* Jessica cried, stepping into the crowd. She crossed her arms in front of her red-and-white cheerleading sweater, glaring at them with a cold stare of superiority she must have learned from Lila. If there was one thing Jessica despised, it was being called ditzy. "That is the last straw! I am so totally sick of this!"

"Hear, hear!" somebody called.

"Hello! We're playing El Carro in a few days, and nobody's got an ounce of school spirit!" Jessica protested, her practiced cheerleader's voice resonating through the lobby. The crowd quieted to listen. "You boneheads—both groups of boneheads—are wasting your lives, stressing about two morons beating each other up at a dumb dance. Get over it!"

"You can't act like nothing happened," Jan said. "Justin's arm is in a sling!"

"It was his own fault!" Jessica said. "And even if Tad was out of line, he's paying for what he

53

did. He's got detention out the wazoo!"

"Right. Jock detention!" Jan scoffed. "When it's a big, strong football player who's in trouble, Coach gives him special, morning detention just so the team won't lose two-hundred-forty pounds of brute force in after-school practice!"

"A fat lot you know about it!" Claire cried. "Coach is keeping an eagle eye on Blubber at practice. If the poor guy even *thinks* about stepping out of line, he's toast! He—"

"Get a life, all of you!" Jessica yelled. "It happened. So what? It's over. Now it's time for all of us to stand together to support our team!"

A few people clapped, but as Elizabeth scanned the crowd she realized most of the kids still looked angry. To her relief the first homeroom bell rang, and the crowd began to scatter.

"Boy, am I glad you showed up!" Elizabeth said, patting her sister on the shoulder. "I really thought they were going to get violent."

Jessica laughed. "If they do, I know what side will come out on top! The teeniest basketball player could slam-dunk any one of those burnouts and not even break a sweat!"

"And any one football player could wipe out the whole smoking ramp with a single tackle," Claire said. She and Jessica began walking with

Elizabeth, Enid, and Maria toward their home-room classes.

Elizabeth sighed. "Does Tad know his Steinbeck test score is displayed for public consumption?"

"He knows it, all right," Maria said. "He was in a few minutes before you got here, just after his detention was over for the morning."

"How many freakazoids bit the dust when he saw they posted his test?" Jessica asked, a little too gleefully. "He must have gone ballistic!"

"Old Blubber didn't touch a single greasy, smoke-scented hair on their heads," Maria said. "He took one look at that test paper and bolted, like he was running for his life. He didn't even bother to tear it down."

"He must have been afraid he would lose his cool again if he stuck around," Elizabeth guessed.

Claire sighed. "I feel bad for him. He's got something besides a few heavy-metal songs on his mind. I wish I could find out what it was."

"I hope you find out soon," Enid said grimly, "before the jocks decide it's their turn to get revenge."

Chapter 4

Jessica skipped her third-period French class that day so she could sunbathe in the school courtyard with Lila and Amy. They headed to lunch a few minutes before the bell rang for the end of third period but came to a halt as soon as they stepped inside the nearly empty cafeteria. Along the opposite wall someone had spray-painted a message in big black letters: Die, Wimps, Hippies, Punks, and Brains!

"The jocks got their revenge," Lila said with a laugh.

Jessica was incensed. "I can't believe they're acting so immature!"

Amy raised her perfectly tweezed eyebrows. "Explain the part where this is bad."

"She's right, Jess," Lila pointed out. "You *loathe* wimps, hippies, punks, and brains. All the cool people hate them!"

"That's not the point!" Jessica cried. "This whole turf war is juvenile! Nobody's paying attention to important things anymore, like having fun and flirting with cute guys and getting ready for the football game this week!"

Lila shook her head slowly. "You are so shallow."

"You yourself complained that the boys aren't gaga over your new baby doll dress today," Jessica pointed out. "What do you suppose they're thinking about instead?"

"You have a point," Lila admitted, smoothing the polka-dotted skirt with her hand. "This dress is way sexy on me. The guys must be too busy proving their manhood to each other to notice."

"Their priorities are totally fatal," Amy said. "Though I approve of their choice of enemies. Those hippies and freaks are too weird."

Other students were filing into the cafeteria by now. As they walked in, most stopped abruptly, as Jessica had, and stared at the writing on the wall. She and her friends hurried to get into the cafeteria line before the others and then snagged their favorite table. A few minutes later

Todd and Maria Slater settled in at the adjacent table, followed by Winston and Maria Santelli.

"Toddy boy," Jessica said. "Where's your better half?"

"Elizabeth's meeting me here in a few minutes," he replied. "But some people would say she's *your* better half."

Winston gave him a thumbs-up signal. "Score one for the Toddster!"

"Speaking of Wakefields, your mother is an interior designer, Jess," Maria Slater said. "What would she think of the new decorating scheme in here?" She nodded toward the spray-painted scrawls.

Maria Santelli stood for a moment to rearrange the pleats of her scarlet cheerleading skirt. "This decorating scheme is a vast improvement over the one in the front lobby this morning," she responded. "That was a low trick, posting Tad's test score for the whole school to see!"

"I sure wouldn't want to find my grade up there," Jessica admitted.

"Did you blow chunks on that Steinbeck thing too?" Amy asked.

Jessica shrugged. "How was I supposed to know *Tortilla Flat* wasn't about a Mexican restaurant?"

Todd rolled his eyes. "You were supposed to read the book."

"As in every single page?" Jessica asked. "Yeah, right! Are you totally wiggy?"

"Speaking of wiggy, here comes Chrome Dome Cooper," Maria Slater said, pointing with one long, graceful hand. "What do you think he'll recommend this time—the firing squad or the guillotine?"

The principal stood in the doorway as if frozen there, and his lips tightened as he stared at the freshly painted graffiti. The roar of voices in the cafeteria dulled as everyone awaited his reaction.

"I've never seen Chrome Dome turn such an interesting shade of purple before," Winston reflected. "Even his bald, shiny little head is sort of a red-violet."

To Jessica's surprise the principal spun on his heel and stormed off without a word, and the buzz of voices in the cafeteria rose again. A few minutes later, as Elizabeth slid into the seat next to Todd, the PA system rumbled to life.

"Attention, all students," crackled Mr. Cooper's formal, stilted voice over the loud-speaker. *"At some undetermined time this morning a grievous act of vandalism occurred in our school cafeteria. . . ."*

"Please!" Winston begged. "Not Antivandalism Lecture Number Sixty-three!"

"It isn't fair for him to nag at us during lunch," Jessica complained. "We get nagged at all day long during classes. There should be something in the Bill of Rights about the right to a nag-free lunch."

"E-mail the White House," Elizabeth suggested.

"Why did he run off to his office to use the public-address system instead of lecturing us in person when he was here a minute ago?" Todd asked.

"He probably wanted to speak to the whole student body at once, not just those of us who have lunch right now," Maria Santelli guessed.

". . . *destructive behavior not befitting young men and women of such caliber as we have here at Sweet Valley High* . . ." the principal droned on.

"Have you heard the latest about Blubber?" Amy asked.

Winston jumped from his seat and made a deep bow in front of her. "No, your Royal Gossipness, we haven't been blessed with that particular dirt. Enlighten us, please!"

"What is it with you, Egbert?" Amy asked. "Do you have some deep-seated childhood trauma?"

Jessica pretended to swat him with her lunch

tray. "Down, boy," she ordered. "Let the Queen of Inside Information speak."

". . . *I assure you,*" continued Mr. Cooper, "*I will find the responsible parties, and when I do . . .*"

Amy paused for dramatic effect, and Jessica rolled her eyes. Amy adored being the first to pass on any new rumor. Finally she spoke. "I just heard from a very reliable source that Tad was seen going into the school guidance office for counseling!"

"Big deal," scoffed Lila. "Lots of kids go to the guidance counselor. Maybe he wanted information on taking his SATs."

"That wasn't why," Amy said knowingly.

"Tad Johnson couldn't *spell* SAT," Maria Slater put in.

"I am getting so sick of these 'dumb jock' jokes—" Todd said, scowling.

"I also heard," Amy continued, talking over his voice as if nobody else had spoken, "that the English test isn't the only one Blubber has screwed up in the last month or two."

"That's not exactly a revelation," Lila said. "Tad's a nice guy, but everyone knows his biceps are bigger than his brain."

"This is different," Amy said. "His grade-point average is totally on the critical list."

Todd stared at her. "Are you talking academic probation? As in not being allowed to play sports until his grades go up?"

"He's not quite to that point yet," Amy said. "But according to my sources, he could be soon. If Blubber doesn't hit the books fast, his high-school football career will be circling the bowl."

Winston whistled and put an arm around Maria Santelli. "That's harsh, man!"

"It's the rule," Maria replied. "What a blow to Tad! He *lives* for football!"

"And El Carro's got an awesome new quarter-back," Jessica said. "We need Tad on defense this week—and we need him focused on the game! Couldn't Mr. Collins have waited to give him back his test until next week?"

"Right," Elizabeth said. "Why let a little thing like classes get in the way of tossing around a funny-shaped ball and ramming yourself into people?"

"I thought you liked football games!" Todd exclaimed.

Elizabeth sighed. "I do. I'm sorry, I didn't mean . . ."

Her voice trailed off as Mr. Cooper drew to a close. "*I will tolerate no further acts of vandalism on the campus of Sweet Valley High. This will not happen again!*"

"He's too late," Elizabeth announced. "It already has."

Amy practically pounced. "What are you talking about?"

"I was just in the girls' locker room. Somebody scrawled all over the mirrors with lipstick."

"I'm afraid to ask what they wrote," Maria Slater said.

Elizabeth glanced warily at Jessica. "It says, 'Cheerleaders have pom-poms for brains.'"

Jessica drew in a sharp breath and then measured out her words through clenched teeth. "I have only one thing to say to that," she began. She narrowed her eyes at the spray-painted message on the wall. *"Die, wimps, hippies, punks, and brains!"*

Olivia entered her favorite VHO chat room and scanned the list of screen names to see who was tuned in. Early evening was prime time for high-school students to hang out in cyberspace—the chat room was nearly full. Quarter wasn't there, but Olivia's friends ChitCat and JohnnyB were on-line, as well as several other kids she'd come to know in cyberspace.

"Man, am I glad to be here with you all!"

Olivia typed. *"It sure is simpler than the off-line world."*

"You said it, Free!" JohnnyB replied. *"On-line, everything is clean and uncomplicated."*

"And if somebody flames you, you can escape to a different chat room!" concluded ChitCat.

"Flames?" asked a first-time chat participant, or "newbie," named Bookworm.

"Flaming is Internet lingo for ranting obnoxiously on-line," Olivia explained. *"The worst flamers do it in all-capital letters."* Aloud she added to herself, "Kind of like 'Die, wimps, hippies, punks, and brains!'" Unfortunately real life offered no alternative lunchrooms to escape to. The different factions of students at Sweet Valley High were stuck with each other.

The public posting of Tad's test paper in the lobby that morning had set off a chain of incidents. The words on the cafeteria wall and the lipstick-scribbled insult to cheerleaders only led to more sneak attacks. Someone threw a smoke bomb onto the smoking ramp right after lunch. Between fifth and sixth period Olivia opened her locker to find a card printed with the slogan, Make Peace, Not Football. Somebody— probably Keith and his friends, she guessed—slipped the cards into every locker in the building.

An incensed Principal Cooper called an assembly

at the end of the day to denounce the vandalism and clique rivalries. But when students filed out of the auditorium afterward and headed outside, they found the words Fashion Queens = Ice Princesses spray-painted on one wall of the school.

The tension hadn't ended with the last bell of the day. In the Dairi Burger parking lot after school Bruce Patman picked a fight with Max Dellon, the motorcycle-riding lead guitarist for the Droids. Neither boy was hurt, but an hour later Bruce found the tires of his Porsche slashed. Olivia had fled the Dairi Burger in disgust.

That had been an hour ago. Now she was on-line, and the bad vibes were behind her for the day. As she chatted with her virtual friends Olivia could feel her pulse slowing and the tense lines in her forehead smoothing themselves out. "Only one thing would improve my mood right now." She spoke aloud, staring at the list of chat participants' names on her screen. "It'd be great if that guy Quarter showed up again."

Wait a minute! she suddenly thought. *Quarter could just as easily be a girl!*

It was funny, Olivia realized. For some reason she'd assumed Quarter was a boy, but now she replayed the conversation in her mind and realized Quarter hadn't said anything that would give her a clue either way. She hoped Quarter was a guy. It was hard not to think of romance when she'd been feeling so alone lately. But even if her new friend was a girl, she was a welcome friend, Olivia told herself. Quarter was sweet and funny, with a sense of humor and a genuine interest in what Olivia thought and felt. Those were traits she'd value in a female pal as well as a boyfriend.

Then she laughed at herself. It was a little early to be thinking in terms of boyfriends. She'd only talked to Quarter once, and they'd never met in person.

What do I really know about Quarter? she thought. He or she had asked if any El Carro students were on-line, so Olivia figured Quarter must be from El Carro too. It was only a few miles from Sweet Valley High. Maybe her path and Quarter's had crossed before! She wondered if she could have seen him—or her—at an academic competition, like a science fair or the regional spelling bee, or at the beach or the mall.

Suddenly the name Quarter popped up on the list of participants on her screen, as if its user had sensed her thoughts.

"Hey, Free and company!" Quarter said, joining the conversation on-line. *"How's everyone's*

Tuesday going?"

"*Much better now!*" Olivia typed impulsively. She blushed, though there was nobody there to see. "*I mean, it's better now that I'm being virtual instead of live and in person.*"

"*I'm glad you're here, Freeverse,*" Quarter said. "*What's a fellow got to do to talk to you alone for a few minutes?*"

"*How about a private chat room?*" Olivia keyed in. She grinned broadly. A fellow? Quarter was a he all right. And he wanted to be alone with her! OK, she reminded herself, he wanted to be alone with her in a cyberspace chat room, not in a car parked at Miller's Point, Sweet Valley's favorite make-out spot. But it was a start.

Quarter and Freeverse took leave of the crowd in the public room and moved into a separate conversation. "*What did you want to talk to me about?*" Olivia asked. She felt a stab of anxiety. What if he just wanted her help on an English paper?

"*I have a cyberpresent for you,*" said Quarter. "*I didn't want to give it to you with a dozen people listening in.*"

Olivia was mystified. "*A cyberpresent? I've never heard of such a thing.*"

"I just coined the term."

"I knew you were lying when you said you were no good at English!"

"The thing is, I was passing a beautiful field of flowers on the way home from school, and I picked one for you," Quarter said.

"That's so sweet!"

"I'm clueless about names of flowers, but I'll describe it to you," Quarter said. "Imagine I'm holding it out in my hand, reaching toward yours. Are you with me?"

"I'm into it," said Olivia. "What color is the flower?"

"It's a bright, passionate red," he told her, "the reddest red you can ever imagine. Vivid, like the pictures you paint with words."

Olivia was wowed. "Tell me more!"

"Its petals are as thin as tissue paper, fragile. But they're soft and warm. And inside, there are these black thready things. The red and black together are awesome. Contrast, I guess you artists would call it."

"It sounds like a poppy! I love poppies!"

"Yeah, I think you're right. I think that's the name. And I love them too. Do you have it in your hand now?"

"Yes, I'm holding it between my fingers.

68

Thank you!" Olivia replied. *"This is amazing, Quarter. I can practically feel those tissue-thin petals."*

"So you like your cyberpresent?"

"It's the best cyberpresent in the whole world!"

"Or at least in cyberspace," Quarter reminded her.

Olivia sighed. She'd never met anyone like Quarter; he had a way of making her feel—well, special. Why couldn't the boys she knew at Sweet Valley High be so warm and open?

Chapter 5

Something slapped against Ken's bare shoulder, stinging. He whirled to see Danny Porter laughing at him. The towel Danny had just snapped at Ken still dangled from his hand. Wednesday's football practice was over, and the team was in the boys' locker room, getting dressed.

"Spill the beans, Matthews!" Danny demanded, straddling a bench between two rows of lockers. "You've been grinning like a crazy man all through football practice. What's up?"

"He's right, Ken," Michael Lewis observed. "You're way too happy! You weren't even phased by that bonehead, burnout prankster setting off the sprinklers and drenching us during drills!"

Ken rolled his eyes. "What's the point of getting mad? It was a lame trick, but I guess it was payback for whoever stole Justin's flannel shirt from his locker and ran it up the flagpole this morning."

Danny laughed. "That one was classic! I wish I'd thought of it."

"Too bad Justin wasn't still in his shirt at the time," Michael said. "What a creep! I bet he was the one who painted Dumb Jock down the front of Blubber's locker."

Ken gazed across the room at Tad, who was sitting silently in the corner, yanking a pair of Nike athletic shoes onto his feet with tense, jerky motions. His brother, Zack, was leaning over him, talking softly, but Tad kept shaking his head. "I wish the idiots would lay off him," Ken said. "Blubber's had about as much as he can take."

"Filling his helmet with water was a sucky thing to do," Danny said, balling one hand into a fist. "Just give me ten minutes alone with whoever's pulling that kind of stuff!"

"It does seem like someone ought to knock some sense into these freaks," Michael agreed.

"Chrome Dome's going to throw the book at anyone he catches—if he catches anyone," Ken said.

"But in the meantime all he can do is have

71

every bit of graffiti painted over," Danny pointed out. "Fat lot of good that does! Erasing the words won't stop Blubber from obsessing about them."

"The Blub was stressed enough before they started going after him," Michael said. "I'm surprised he hasn't had a major blowout this week. I know I would!"

"He will if he doesn't talk to someone," Ken said in a low, tense voice.

For a few minutes the boys dressed in silence. "Matthews, you still haven't told us why you've had that dopey grin on your face all through practice!" Michael said finally as he pulled a duffel bag from his locker and stuffed his practice clothes into it.

Ken shrugged innocently. "No reason. I'm just high on football, I guess."

"Maybe El Carro's new quarterback is moving to South America before Friday," Michael suggested.

"In my dreams," said Ken, pulling a polo shirt from his duffel bag and sliding it over his damp blond hair.

Danny shook his head. "It's a girl," he decided, eyeing Ken carefully. "It's got to be a girl. You're holding out on us, Matthews. You met someone!"

"Who, me?" Ken said. "Where would I meet somebody? I spend my whole life in class, at football practice, and sitting alone in my room with my computer." He hid a spontaneous grin by turning to his locker and burying his head in his backpack. He'd talked to Freeverse on-line again Tuesday night, after his parents thought he was sleeping. And they'd had another chat this morning before school.

"Then it's someone you already knew," Danny persisted, pulling him back to the real world.

"You know everyone I know," Ken said.

"I saw you dancing with Lila Fowler at the dance last weekend," Michael said, wiggling his eyebrows comically. "She's a babe—and rich too. I bet you're hot for her!"

Ken grimaced and was glad that the locker room had mostly cleared out by now. "Not in this lifetime!"

"Speaking of babes, I heard a certain cheer-leading cocaptain practicing a special cheer today, Danny," Michael said. "And it's got your name in it!"

Danny blushed. "Aw, lay off, Lewis. I can't control what the cheerleaders do."

"I've seen you eyeing those Wakefield pom-poms," Michael said. "And you're not the only one in the offensive lineup who worships the ground she cheers on!"

This time Danny scowled. "I can't control Bryce Fisherman's hormones either."

Michael laughed, and Ken joined in. Finally, he realized, he didn't feel the least bit uncomfortable hearing Michael joke about Jessica flirting with his teammates. Freeverse had made all the difference.

"Come on, QB," Danny urged, changing the subject. "Who's the mystery woman? Didn't you see the rule in the playbook about not hiding anything from your teammates?"

"I must have missed that one."

"Someone else missed it too," Michael said, his voice suddenly serious. Ken followed his gaze. Zack was gone, and Tad was sitting across the room, alone, his head in his hands. If Ken hadn't known Tad so well, he'd have sworn the big linebacker was struggling to hold back tears.

Jessica stood on the sidelines Friday afternoon, leading the cheerleaders in some warm-up cheers while students filled the stands of Sweet Valley High's stadium.

Football games ranked high on Jessica's list of favorite things in the world. The evening wouldn't be dark until well into the game, but the stadium lights were already on, glaring a startling, garish white that lent the whole scene the air of a carnival. The marching band was playing, a cool breeze ruffled Jessica's hair, and the air smelled of nachos and anticipation. This same heady thrill coursed through her body every time she performed in front of a lot of people, and Jessica never tired of the adrenaline rush.

Even the "away" side of the bleachers was packed, the rows of filled seats dappled with El Carro's orange and black. To Jessica's practiced ear it was clear that the Cougars' upset of Compton the weekend before had energized the El Carro fans. They were wild with excitement.

The energy level on the Sweet Valley side of the stadium was also high, but it seemed to Jessica that the energy wasn't all positive. Practically the entire school was massing there, even the apathetic kids—like some of Jan and Justin's crowd—who seldom turned out for football games. Jessica wanted to believe it meant school spirit was alive and well at Sweet Valley High, but she was afraid it really meant trouble. The War of the Cliques had been intensifying all week, leaving everyone angry and keyed up.

She could hear a hard, cold edge on the buzz of voices coming from the SVH stands.

Well, if anyone can change that, it's me! Jessica decided firmly. "All right, cheerleaders!" she called to the squad. "We need to remind this crowd that Sweet Valley rules supreme! Let's build some school spirit!" She launched into a cartwheel, and some of the other cheerleaders followed suit. "It's time to practice some of those new cheers!" she suggested loudly to spur some interest in the stands. "Give 'em a preview of what to expect during the game!"

Heather Mallone, her cheerleading cocaptain, stepped forward and shrugged her thick mane of curly blond hair behind her shoulders. "Ready, girls?" she asked in a commanding tone.

Jessica clenched her teeth. She hated it when her cocaptain took control of the squad, but making a scene about it in front of the entire student body was no way to build school spirit.

Heather assumed what Jessica thought of as The Position. "Hands on hips, smiles on lips!" the tall, shapely senior sang out. Heather had moved to town from Nevada that year and had incensed Jessica by nearly usurping her cheerleading squad. Eventually they'd learned to work together, but Heather's take-charge attitude and singsong voice still irritated Jessica like fingernails on a chalkboard.

"We'll start with the Bryce Fisherman cheer," Heather mandated. Jessica nodded, relieved. The cheerleaders had created personalized cheers for most of the players, with Jessica herself writing and choreographing cheers for Bryce and Danny. If Heather had to lead the first cheer, well, at least she'd chosen one of Jessica's.

Jessica smiled her most dazzling smile and glanced down the line to be sure the girls were in position. Then, with Heather leading, the squad launched into Jessica's cheer:

When Bryce runs the ball,
he's an awesome sight.
It's another TD
for the red and white!

Heather leaped into her flashy signature jump, a triple herky and Y-leap combination. As always, Jessica had to admit that one of the most annoying things about Heather was that she really was a terrific cheerleader. *But not better than me!* Jessica reminded herself. To prove it, she executed a no-hands cartwheel and landed it in a split. Then, before Heather could object, she took charge of the next practice cheer:

> When we need a first down
> and we need it fast,
> Danny is the man
> who will catch that pass!

The kickoff was a few minutes away, so it was time for player introductions. The game announcer's voice crackled over the loudspeaker, calling the names of the El Carro Cougars one by one while fans on the far side of the stadium clapped and whistled. Then it was the Gladiators' turn.

Michael Lewis was the first player to run onto the field, and applause erupted from the Sweet Valley stands. The cheerleaders vaulted into stag leaps and double herkies, waving their red-and-white pom-poms to whip up excitement. One at a time the other defensive players jogged into view.

"And rounding out the Gladiators' defensive line," called the announcer, "at six-foot two and two-hundred-forty pounds, wearing jersey twenty-one, is Tad 'Blubber' Johnson!"

Tad charged onto the field, revved up and clearly ready to work out a ton of frustration. *After the grief he's been getting all week, I sure wouldn't want to be the Cougar who gets in Blubber's way tonight!* Jessica thought as she shook her pom-poms over her head.

Something made her look up into the crowd as Tad ran past her. The tone and volume of the fans' cheering had changed; suddenly it was half-hearted, as if some students didn't care to welcome the linebacker onto the field. Jessica motioned for the cheerleaders to take up the slack, leaping higher and cheering louder for Tad. But her heart thudded to her sneakers. Those were catcalls she was hearing from the stands—and from Tad's own classmates!

Nicky Shepard jumped to his feet in the front row of the bleachers. His black T-shirt with the logo of a heavy-metal band stood out starkly from the red-and-white shirts of the fans around him.

"Hey, Blubber!" Nicky jeered when the linebacker was only a few feet away from him. *"The twenty-one on your shirt is your IQ, right? What are your parents: Cro-Magnon or Neanderthal?"*

Tad froze, the color of his face deepening to a dark, ominous red. Suddenly he launched himself into the stands like a torpedo and began pummeling Nicky. The smaller boy went down, blood spurting from his nose. Still Tad kept throwing punches. It took four of his teammates and Coach Schultz to pull him off Nicky's still form.

Jessica could hardly believe what was happening. Security guards escorted Tad to the field house. Then everyone looked on, amid stunned whispers, as a rescue squad crew loaded the pale, unconscious Nicky onto a stretcher. In a daze Jessica watched both coaches gesturing excitedly as they spoke with the officials on the sidelines. Coach Schultz's face was as white as the team jerseys, but he also looked furious—as furious as Tad had been.

A few minutes later the ambulance roared off, siren shrieking, with Nicky in the back.

"Attention, ladies and gentlemen!" the game announcer's voice blared over the public-address system. The excited jabbering of the crowd softened to a hush. "This game is now officially over!" the announcer said. "Sweet Valley High forfeits to El Carro."

Chapter 6

"Tad has totally lost it," Elizabeth said forty minutes later as she sat at Casey's Ice Cream Parlor with Jessica and Todd. Most of their friends were congregating at the Dairi Burger or Guido's Pizza, but neither of the twins was in the mood for a crowd scene. "I can't believe what a monster he's turned into!"

Across the table from her Jessica dropped her spoon. "And I can't believe you're sticking up for that slimeball Nicky Shepard! He had no right saying such a lousy thing. He's the monster, not Tad!"

"Nicky was mean," Elizabeth agreed, gesturing with a spoonful of hot fudge sundae, "but that's no excuse for beating him unconscious!"

"I'm sorry he got hurt, but it was his own fault."

"Just a few days ago you were ticked off at both sides for fighting at the dance and acting so juvenile all week," Elizabeth reminded her. "Including Tad and his friends!"

"That was different!" Jessica insisted. "Tad was out of line at the dance, and he's paying for it. But you heard what Nicky said to him tonight! It was way harsh!"

"No harsher than being pounded into the bleachers!" Elizabeth shot back. She turned to Todd, who was sitting beside her, expecting him to support her argument. But his eyes were fixed on his banana split.

Jessica's eyes flashed with anger and frustration. "Besides, half the school has treated Blubber like dirt all week! How much is the poor guy supposed to put up with?"

"I don't blame Tad for having his feelings hurt or even for being mad," Elizabeth said. "But violence never solved anything! He should have found another way to deal with it."

"Oh, sure," Jessica countered. "That's realistic. Even before the dance he was already freaking out about something, according to the guys on the team. Then he gets picked on all week long, and Coach gives him mega-detention, and he's bungee jumping toward academic probation—"

Elizabeth shook her head. "Todd, don't you think—" she interrupted, but Jessica kept on talking.

"Then a loser like Nicky disses him big-time in front of hundreds of people," Jessica said, her voice rising. "And you expect Blubber to turn the other cheek and say, 'Thank you, Freak Face, can I have another?'"

"Anything's better than jumping the guy like a maniac!" Elizabeth cried. "Especially since Tad is so much bigger than Nicky."

"I don't like violence either," Jessica declared, pounding her fist on the table. "But sometimes there's no choice! Sometimes you have to fight for your rights—for your self-respect!"

"You just don't get it, Jessica! Tad lost control, and now a boy is lying in the hospital. He could be seriously injured!"

Jessica rolled her eyes. "Lighten up, Liz. I'm sure El Creepo will be fine."

"Lighten up?" Elizabeth cried in disbelief. "This isn't just 'bleeding heart Elizabeth' rooting for the underdog! We're talking about a criminal offense. Tad could be charged with assault!"

"Why? Nobody in their right mind would blame him for what happened!"

"Oh, so now I'm not in my right mind!" Elizabeth said, louder. "I suppose you have to be a jock to be considered sane these days." The ice cream parlor was nearly empty, but a few customers were nudging each other and staring. Elizabeth closed her eyes and took a deep breath, then continued in a quieter, controlled tone. "Todd, you're an athlete; maybe my psycho sister will listen to you. Tell her that not all jocks are violent bullies with no self-control."

Todd looked up, blinking as he glanced from one twin to the other. "Well, it's true that fighting isn't always a good idea," he faltered.

Elizabeth stared at him. "That's a blinding flash of the obvious."

"I mean, I wish the whole thing hadn't happened," Todd said carefully. "It's too bad Nicky got hurt and the game got canceled."

"In other words, you agree with me," Jessica said triumphantly. "You wish it hadn't happened, but you think Blubber was justified!"

"Well, uh, I didn't say th-that, exactly," Todd stammered, glancing nervously at Elizabeth.

She stared at him sharply. "What are you trying

not to say, Todd? Are you condoning what Tad did to Nicky?"

"Yes, I guess I am," he admitted.

Elizabeth scowled. "Boys will be boys, right?"

"Told you so!" Jessica sang out.

"How can you stick up for that bully?" Elizabeth demanded.

"Liz, I don't like violence either. But for once in her life, Jessica is right. Nicky started it. He was just as violent as Tad, but he was violent with his words instead of his fists. You're the one who's always saying how powerful words can be!"

"Then Tad should've written a letter to the editor!" Elizabeth cried. "You actually believe that saying something mean is just as bad as a physical assault?"

"Yes, in some cases it is," Todd said.

"So much for sticks and stones," Elizabeth said, disgusted. "What's really going on here is that you're both sticking up for Tad because you're jocks, taking the jocks' side!"

"That isn't fair!" Todd cried.

"And beating up Nicky was?"

"He had it coming," Jessica insisted.

"Nobody deserves to be knocked senseless!"

"If you ask me, he didn't have much sense to begin with," Todd said bitterly.

"I can't believe I'm hearing this!" Elizabeth exclaimed. She jumped to her feet, grabbing the keys to the Jeep from where they lay on the table in front of Jessica. "I'm leaving, Jessica. If you want a ride, come on. Otherwise you can ask your jock friend to drop you off," she said, glaring at Todd. "After all, you athletic types always stick together."

Jessica followed her out wordlessly, and the twins rode home together in stony silence.

Ken logged onto VHO as soon as he arrived home from the disastrous football game, hoping to find Freeverse in their usual chat room. He sympathized with Tad's anger and frustration, but he wished his friend had found a less violent way of dealing with his emotions. And he was ticked off about having to forfeit the game. He'd been psyched to play El Carro. Now he'd never know if he could have beaten the Cougars' new quarterback.

"Aw, rats!" he said aloud as the list of current chat-room participants bloomed in the corner of his screen. Freeverse wasn't on it. But he grinned a minute later when her screen name suddenly appeared. It seemed as if she were logging on in response to his wishful thinking.

"Did you hear what happened tonight at the football game between SVH and El Carro?" he asked after they greeted each other.

"Yeah, I heard." Her words popped onto his screen. *"But I've got to confess, I go to the rival school."*

Ken was surprised for a moment—not because Freeverse went to El Carro but because she seemed to know that he went to Sweet Valley. He realized he must have let something slip about his school in one of their earlier conversations. *"Oops!"* he said. *"I hope that's not the kiss of death for our cyberconversations!"*

"School sports rivalries don't matter to me, Quarter," Freeverse responded. *"I sometimes go to football games. But I'm not wild about them. Football is too aggressive and violent! I'd rather take a stroll along the shoreline any day!"*

Ken bit his lip. He certainly couldn't tell her exactly who he was at Sweet Valley High. Luckily, he realized, she'd provided him with an easy out—a quick way to change the subject. *"Today would be a great day for walking on the beach and visiting all those seagulls!"* he typed.

"So why don't we do it now?" Freeverse suggested.

Ken yanked his hands away from the keyboard.

"Uh-oh," he said out loud. "What do I do now?"

He reviewed the situation in his head. *I like this girl,* he told himself. *Or I think I do.* But what if they didn't hit it off when they met in person? Or what if he liked her, but Freeverse couldn't stand him? *I mean, come on,* he thought, *she doesn't even like football—she thinks football players are aggressive and violent!* She might even recognize him as Sweet Valley High's quarterback, or they might run into somebody who knew him. Then where would he be?

Finally he admitted that something else had him worried: *What if she's, well . . . unattractive?* he asked himself. *Call me shallow, but I couldn't deal with that! It would be totally fatal to our chances of being more than on-line correspondents.*

He also had to consider a more serious issue. Freeverse might not be what she seemed at all. He'd heard about adults on the Internet, preying on kids and teens by pretending to be something they weren't. Freeverse could be some psycho trying to get Ken onto a private strip of beach.

Suddenly Ken wanted to hit the escape key, exit VHO, and switch off his power supply.

He looked back at his screen and realized Freeverse had typed another line: *"Of course, I mean a cyberwalk."*

Ken sighed deeply and then laughed at his own indecision. "Of course!" he said to his monitor. "A virtual walk."

He'd paused for so long that he thought she must be wondering if she'd scared him off. *"Sorry for the delay,"* he typed quickly. *"My mother was asking me something. A walk on the beach sounds awesome! How do we get there?"*

"I'll snag a private chat room," Freeverse replied, *"and then I'll meet you there! Stay tuned for directions to the beach!"*

"It's a date!" Ken keyed in.

"A warm, gentle breeze feathers the sand as the late afternoon sun dances a sparkling path over blue-green waves," Olivia typed as she waited in the private chat room for the boy from El Carro to navigate his way there. She wasn't sure how to plan a cyberwalk on the beach, but setting the stage with description seemed like a logical first step.

Olivia was startled at her own temerity for suggesting the virtual stroll. But that was the beauty of cyberspace—she could try on unfamiliar behaviors, risk-free. And asking a guy she didn't know to walk with her on a virtual beach was certainly unfamiliar! She hoped Quarter didn't think she was too flaky or too serious or too much of a nerd. But the truth was, she didn't know what he thought of her—except that he kept coming back for more conversation, so he must not think she was *too* uncool. She thought about the virtual poppy he'd given her, and she decided to go on describing the beach scene exactly as she saw it in her head.

"Farther down the beach a few people are playing and sunbathing, their suits scribbled in crayon colors on tawny dunes. But our own stretch of sand is empty, wide, and soft. Seagulls wheel overhead in a clear, thin sky, their calls punctuating the constant whoosh of sea against sand."

A window opened on her screen, alerting her that Quarter had just entered the room. She greeted him. After a few seconds he answered. *"Wow! What an excellent day! Great surf too. I love big waves."*

Olivia closed her eyes for a moment and smiled. He didn't sound like someone who thought she was flaky. She concentrated hard on imagining herself there on the beach with a nameless, faceless boy walking beside her. She could almost feel the wind messing up her curly hair; she could practically hear the crash of waves. *"I love big waves too,"* she told Quarter through her keyboard. *"Nothing makes me feel the way the ocean does. Relaxed, alive, and free. It's a healing place, almost magical."*

"I know exactly what you mean," Quarter replied, *"though my friends would think I was turning into a dweeb if I tried to explain it to them! At my school it's socially unacceptable to think too much about anything besides parties and games."*

"Oh, yes!" Olivia typed forcefully. *"That is so true at my school too! But what would you tell your friends about the ocean if you could?"*

"I can't put these things into words the way you can," Quarter admitted.

"Try," Olivia challenged.

"The ocean is, like, so huge and so beautiful. And all that bigness and that magic you mentioned before, it's powerful enough to make the problems at school seem minor."

Olivia was impressed. Quarter might not be a poet, but he was honest and open, and he had a way of cutting to exactly what was important. *"I feel that way too,"* she said. *"After a rough week at school a stroll by the ocean is just what I need* to get back my perspective. Shall we walk awhile and enjoy the scenery?"

"Sure," Quarter agreed. "*This breeze is great. I can feel it ruffling through my hair.*"

"What color is it?" Olivia asked on a whim.

"*The breeze?*"

"No, silly," she replied, glad he couldn't see that she was blushing. "Your hair. If you don't mind saying, I mean."

"*It's blond. And yours?*"

"Dark brown," she told him. "And curly."

"*I bet those curls look gorgeous, blowing behind you in the wind, wild and free,*" he said.

"That's one thing about a breezy day on the beach," she typed, thinking about her thick, unruly hair. "Nobody can tell when you're having a bad hair day!"

"*Come on, Free. I know you're not one of those girls who obsess about how their hair looks!*"

"*You're right. I'm not. It would be pointless to obsess about it. My hair has a mind of its own! You said 'wild and free,' and it's a good description.*"

Olivia was embarrassed by the turn the conversation had taken, but she was glad she'd had the nerve to ask. She liked the fact that looks were irrelevant on-line. She knew she wasn't classically beautiful, like Lila and the twins. Or striking and exotic, like Maria Slater or Dana. Olivia thought of herself as OK looking, not especially pretty. But she firmly believed that relationships shouldn't be about looks. She didn't care if Quarter was handsome in the traditional sense. She'd felt attracted to plenty of guys who didn't have movie stars' faces and athletes' bodies.

On the other hand, it was easier to imagine a boy walking beside her on the beach if she knew at least a little about his appearance. Now she could envision Quarter with blond hair. The nameless, faceless person was slowly becoming clearer.

"The wind is blowing a lot more than just our hair," Quarter said. *"It's whipping up the water too. Awesome!"*

"I see," she said, picking up his line of thought. *"The waves are sweeping up in graceful curves, like in a Japanese painting. Each one is crested with dazzling white foam."*

"There are surfers out on the waves. They're cruising, fast and graceful. It's almost like dancing. . . . Oops, that guy just wiped out! Splat!"

Olivia giggled. *"Do you surf, Quart?"*

"Yeah, I do," he replied. "I'm not an expert, but it's a kick now and then. What about you?"

"No," she admitted. "On one hand, it looks like it might feel like flying. But when it came down to it, I'd be too self-conscious . . . and probably too klutzy," she added with a rueful smile.

"You could learn," he said. "I know someone who's not an athlete or anything who suddenly decided to become a surfer. My friend learned in just a few weeks and surprised everyone!"

Olivia laughed. "Yeah, I have a friend who did something like that too," she said, thinking of Elizabeth, who had come close to winning a surfing contest after secretly taking lessons. "She told me you don't have to be an Olympic athlete to learn to surf as long as you have a good teacher."

"I'm available for virtual lessons!" Quarter offered.

"Now there's a whole new twist on the term 'Internet surfing'!" Olivia quipped. "Maybe some other time. I didn't bring my virtual surfboard today! :)"

"So what do you like to do on the beach? Besides walking?"

"If I'm alone, I usually bring my sketchbook

or journal, or a novel or book of poems I'm reading," she said. "I know, that must sound dull and unadventurous."

"Not at all! It takes courage to sit on the beach and sketch in the middle of a bunch of people sunbathing and playing volleyball and stuff. Personally I'd drink my suntan lotion before I'd draw pictures where other people might see them! My artistic talents—or lack thereof—are truly scary!"

"Talent is overrated," Olivia replied. "You might never be Rembrandt, but anyone can learn to draw. It just takes careful observation and a lot of practice. Besides, sketchbooks are private. You don't have to show people!"

"Here's something you could draw," Quarter said. "I'm picking up a shell. It's kind of tan on the outside and smooth white around the edges. Inside it's a delicate shade of pink."

"It sounds pretty," she said, almost believing she was actually inspecting a shell in his hand. For an hour they strolled along their own private beach, pointing out the sights, dipping their toes in the water, and telling each other stories. Olivia felt like she'd been transported to cyberparadise. Quarter was easy to talk to and a lot of fun. With every virtual footprint

95

they left in the sand, she knew he was becoming more special to her. It was hard to believe they'd never actually met.

"Oh!" she said suddenly, and then realized she'd spoken out loud instead of through her keyboard. She typed the word instead. *"It's getting late,"* she continued. *"The sun is setting."*

"It's making the surface of the water shimmer with pastel colors," Quarter replied.

Olivia chuckled. *"I meant the real sun, outside my window. Not the virtual one over our beach. But I like your image of the shimmering colors on the water!"*

Quarter replied with a verse: *"I guess I'm a poet and don't even know it!"*

"LOL," Olivia responded with the common abbreviation for laughing out loud.

"It is getting late," Quarter said. *"I should go. But I hate to say good-bye. This has been great."*

"Yes, it's been a really special time."

"I hope we can do it again," he said. *"Good night, Freeverse."*

"Good night, Quarter."

Reluctantly Olivia exited the chat room and logged off her machine. For several minutes she sat there, staring at the dark screen. Finally she forced herself to stand up from her desk and shake off the cyberdust. *Or sand*, she thought with a smile.

"Good night, Quarter," she said softly to the darkening room. She could have sworn she heard a seagull cry out in reply.

Chapter 7

Ken stood in line in gym class Monday afternoon, waiting for his turn to practice basketball layups. He watched absentmindedly as Barry Rork jogged forward, tossed the ball, and aced the basket. Meanwhile Olivia Davidson was running up from the head of the girls' line. She caught the ball a little awkwardly and leaped into the air in a focused effort to make the basket, but the ball bounced off the rim. Next in line was a scrawny red-haired boy Ken had hardly ever noticed. He tugged at his ill-fitting shorts and moved forward to catch the ball as the class exercise continued.

Ken wasn't thinking about basketball drills. He was thinking about Freeverse. Gym teachers usually discouraged daydreaming, but both teachers who were in charge of Ken's class were busy. The girls' teacher had a special practice with the field hockey team, and Coach Schultz was meeting with someone in his office, just off the gym, with the office door ajar so he could listen for any problems. Ken was glad to have both teachers out of the way. Usually he liked gym class, but today his mind kept straying. He was glad it was the last period of the school day.

Ken had spent much of the weekend daydreaming about Freeverse, and he'd spent even more time chatting with her on-line. He'd neglected his homework, begged off from a family outing, and even forgotten to check the sports scores. His parents complained that he was tying up the phone line with his constant Internet use. But he couldn't help himself. Freeverse made him feel, well, free.

Now he found himself imagining what she looked like. He knew she had curly brown hair and that she didn't think she was pretty. *What if she really is unattractive?* he worried. He decided it probably wasn't an issue. Most girls seemed to hate their looks or at least claimed to. Jessica and Lila were different—not that there was anything to hate about their faces or figures.

But if you told any other attractive girl she had a gorgeous body, she'd say she needed to lose fifteen pounds. If you complimented her on her hair, she'd say it was too long or too short or not the right color. Women were weird that way.

Of course Freeverse must be cute, he told himself, *even if she doesn't think so.* She was a beautiful person on the inside; surely that would show through on the outside.

Something hurled toward him, and a subconscious reflex jerked Ken's hands up to catch the basketball before it slammed into his chest.

"Vegging out, Matthews?" asked Claire, who'd just lobbed it at him. "Your turn for layups."

Ken blinked. "Uh, sorry," he said, springing forward and tossing the ball in the general direction of the net. He missed it completely, and a chorus of catcalls rang out, mostly from the boys' line. Ken's friends were just teasing him, but the guys from some of the rival factions had nasty smirks on their faces. Ken wasn't worried. He was sure the open door to Coach Schultz's office would keep the class under control.

"What's this?" asked Justin. "The Superjock misses a basket?" Until his sprained wrist healed, Justin was standing on the sidelines watching gym class instead of taking part.

"Superjocks don't tax themselves for just anyone," Keith Wagner explained. "After all, there are no college scouts in the stands."

Ken ignored them both.

"Earth to Ken!" Todd called as Jessica expertly shot a basket and then took a dramatic, graceful bow. "The lights are on in there, Matthews," Todd said. "Is anyone home?"

Ken grinned ruefully at his best friend. "I guess I kind of zoned."

Todd, the star forward for the basketball team, sprang forward and slam-dunked the ball.

"Show-off!" Ken called over his shoulder as he jogged to the end of the line with Todd following him.

"Gotta keep you football players on your toes," said Todd. His smile faded. "You OK, man?"

"Me? I'm cool. I'm golden."

"You've never missed a practice layup in your life!" Todd objected, but his eyes darted toward the basket as he spoke. It was Elizabeth's turn to make the shot. Todd watched her with his jaw clenched, but his brown eyes looked sad. Ken knew they'd quarreled about what happened at the El Carro game.

"There's a first time for everything," Ken said. Todd had no idea how true that was. *How's this for a first time?* he asked himself. Ken Matthews—star quarterback, golfer, baseball fanatic, basketball enthusiast, hockey fan, and all-around sports nut—was falling for a girl who couldn't care less about playing to win. In Freeverse's world a puck was a Shakespearean elf, a pigskin was what kept a pig from falling apart, and Cardinals and Orioles were merely colorful birds.

Sports were everything to Ken—especially football. He had never exactly lied to Freeverse, but he had avoided the issue—while pretending to be as open with her as she was with him. He felt guilty about sidestepping around the one thing that had always been the major passion of his life. "The fact is, I'm a total jock," he said under his breath. Freeverse could never really know him unless she knew that.

Partly he'd hidden it because he was afraid of her reaction. He'd never met anyone like Freeverse, and he wanted her to like him. But also it was because he was having so much fun exploring his new friend's more poetic, cerebral point of view. She'd invited him along on flights of imagination—encouraged him to delve into his own thoughts and ideas. Next to that, throwing a leather ball down a field seemed, well, juvenile.

"Basketball layups are too juvenile for words," Lila complained to Jessica, who stood directly in front of her in the layup line. Jessica saw her roll her eyes as some scrawny, red-haired twerp from the math team threw the ball and missed.

"I don't know about juvenile, but this is way dull," Jessica said as the next girl in line took her turn. "Except for the part about watching cute guys in shorts," she added, cocking her head toward Bryce, who jogged forward, caught the ball, and flipped it into the air. It circled the hoop like water spiraling down a drain. "Excellent shot, Bryce!" she called out, flashing him a smile.

"You are such a tease," Lila said in a low voice. "Just a few minutes ago you were sucking up to Danny."

"So? Can't I like them both?"

"I don't think you like either one!"

"Of course I do," Jessica insisted. "They're both cool and fun and cute. And they keep telling me how gorgeous I am. How could I not like them?"

"But you're not serious about them!"

Jessica shook her head sorrowfully. "Serious? Lila, Lila, Lila, where did your father and I go wrong with our little Lila? Flirting isn't about 'serious.'"

Lila crossed her arms. "This I've got to hear. Tell me—oh, Dating Guru. What is flirting about?"

"It's an exercise, like basketball layups," Jessica explained. "When it's your turn, you throw the ball through the hoop to the next person in the boys' line. If it's Danny, that's great. If it's Bryce, that's great too. The next time your turn comes up, it might be someone completely different!"

Lila put her hands on her hips. "What if it's that red-haired creep with the thick glasses?"

"Then you think fast and switch places with somebody else in line."

Lila laughed. "You're too much!"

"I know," Jessica said happily. "But Danny and Bryce should be thanking me for bringing some light into their drab little football players' lives, especially today."

"How do you figure?"

Jessica glanced around the room. "You know how horrid it's been around school all day," she explained in a more serious tone. "Nobody can believe what happened at the so-called football game Friday!"

"Everyone is shell-shocked," Lila agreed. "Except me, of course. In my case it's post–traumatic stress disorder. Sounds classier."

Jessica rolled her eyes. "This isn't a joke, Li. The whole school has an overwhelming sense of ickiness. And the football team's feeling it worse than anyone."

"They're postal about having to forfeit the game."

"True," Jessica said. "But they're not reacting like I thought they would. I was expecting vandalism or fights—preferably during my French quiz!"

"I haven't heard a single sound bite of anything like trouble," Lila said. "Maybe it'll blow over since everyone knows Nicky's going to be OK." The injured boy had spent Friday night in the hospital, but he'd been released Saturday morning and was expected back at school by the end of the week.

"This is not just going to go away," Jessica warned. "Something's in the air. I can feel it."

"Something's sure crackling between your sister and Todd," Lila said. "Look at Liz over there!

She keeps sneaking glances at him and then looking back down at her cross trainers real quick."

"Elizabeth wants us to hand over the school to the burnouts and hippies and brains, like they should be allowed to get away with saying horrible things like Nicky said to Blubber."

"And let me guess—Todd's bonding with his jock friends on the issue."

"As tight as Dana Larson's leather pants," Jessica said, nodding.

"Are Liz and the Toddster even speaking to each other?"

"Not since Friday," Jessica revealed. "And you know how it goes. When those two are mad at each other, the whole school feels it. It's like the forces of the universe are out of whack. Meteors crash into the earth, oceans boil, volcanos spew—"

"Olivia Davidson walks around with a dopey smile on her face, as if she finally found a guy who could put up with her werditude," Lila added, staring incredulously at the curly-haired girl.

"Exactly," Jessica agreed, wondering if Olivia actually had snagged a man. She'd noticed Olivia's expression all day too. The girl looked as if nothing that was going on around her could touch her. "Anyhow, Elizabeth and Todd being mad at each other proves that something truly heavy and bizarre is in the air—I don't know, like a hurricane is about to strike."

Lila laughed. "Hurricane Jessica!" she told her. "You're up next at the basket."

"As if!" Jessica said, glancing around to be sure the coach was still in his office. "I refuse to get sweaty in gym class in front of boys when there's nobody around to dock my grade if I don't!" She pulled Lila out of line, leaving the basket to the next girl.

"Who's Coach meeting with all this time?" Lila asked. "I thought he said he'd be out in a few minutes."

"I hope he takes his megatime. As long as he's in there, he's leaving us alone!"

"Amy will have the scoop," Lila said. Sure enough, Amy was standing just beside the door to Coach Schultz's office, leaning over as if to tie her tennis shoe. "She's been tying that same shoe for ten minutes."

Jessica nodded knowingly. "Maybe we should go help her with those unruly laces."

A crash from Coach Schultz's office stopped the action on the gym floor. Some of the students resumed layups, uneasily, after a moment. But Ken sprinted toward the door, followed by several of his classmates. Amy, Lila, and Jessica were already standing near the office, their eyes wide. But the door blocked their view of the coach and his companion inside.

"Blubber's in there with Coach," Jessica said in a loud whisper, "and he just threw something across the room!" Amy put a finger in front of her mouth in warning and leaned closer to the door. But the voices inside the office were loud enough to keep the athletic director from hearing the students near his door.

"That's enough, Johnson!" came the coach's voice. "I won't stand for any more of your attitude on this!"

"What's happening?" Ken whispered just outside the door.

"The freak's not even hurt bad!" Tad protested inside the office.

"That's hardly the point," Coach Schultz replied. "You used unnecessary roughness. That boy has a mild concussion, and you could have injured him even more seriously!"

"Coach met with Chrome Dome," Amy murmured, filling Ken in on the details. "They're suspending Tad from school for at least a week and from the football team indefinitely!"

"But they can't do that!" Ken exclaimed, raising his voice.

"But you can't do this!" Tad cried out at exactly the same moment, covering the sound of Ken's words. "The little dirtbag goaded me into it! Every burnout and hippie freak at school goaded me into it!"

"Calm down, Tad," Coach said in a firm but soothing voice. "I know it's been rough, but you were out of bounds. You know we can't condone violence at school events—"

"But—"

"My advice is to take your penalty like a man," the coach continued smoothly. "Spend the week keeping up with your schoolwork and thinking about what you've done."

"But I haven't done jack! None of this was my fault!"

"I've briefed your mother, and she agreed to help you come up with a study plan—" the coach began.

"Leave my parents out of this!" Tad bellowed. "They've got nothing to do with this!"

"In the next week," the coach went on as if Tad hadn't spoken, "we'll be reviewing the case and deciding what other steps need to be taken, if any."

"Can you spell *felony?*" Justin asked in a whisper, a smirk on his face. Ken glared at him and noticed that Claire did too.

"What other steps need to be taken?" Tad asked. "What are you going to do—have me arrested? That's prime, man. That's really prime!"

The coach's voice grew sharper. "An arrest is a distinct possibility!" he said grimly. "Don't you get it, Johnson? You sacked that boy in front of hundreds of spectators. What did you think the punishment would be? A five-yard penalty?"

"Why are you doing this to me?" Tad yelled, his voice sounding close to tears.

"I'm not doing anything to you," the coach said. "You've done it to yourself."

"With the help of every burnout at school," Claire whispered, crossing her arms in front of her.

"And the decision to press charges isn't mine," the coach said. "It rests with the Shepard boy and his parents. And the police."

"But you're the one who's suspending me from the team!" Tad said. "Can't you just suspend me from school and still let me play football?"

"At least he has priorities," Keith whispered dryly.

"We're up against Palisades this week—you

110

need me!" Tad said. "I won't flip out at the next game, Coach. I swear it!"

"The violence alone is enough to strike you out of the athletic program," the coach informed him. "But even if it had never happened, you'd still be off the team!"

"What are you talking about?" Tad demanded.

Jessica gasped. "It's his English grade! It's gotta be his English grade!" she whispered.

"Roger Collins informed me this morning about a certain English paper he graded over the weekend."

"So what if I got an F?" Tad protested. "That assignment reeked. Nobody in their right mind could've done well on it!"

"I got an A," Elizabeth whispered with a shrug.

"Me too," said Olivia, who had just joined the growing crowd at the door.

Jessica stared disdainfully at them both. "As the boy said, 'nobody in their right mind.'"

"Shhh!" Ken hissed.

"Mr. Collins tells me that combined with a test you fumbled last week, this paper puts your English grade in serious jeopardy," the coach said.

"Blubber couldn't even spell *jeopardy*," said the red-haired boy from the math team.

"You're now officially failing English," the coach told Tad. "And your other grades are less than all-star material."

"What does that have to do with football?" Tad protested.

"You know the rules, Tad. You're on academic probation!"

Claire shook her head sadly. "Which means he can't play team sports."

"This must be a joke!" Tad yelled. Ken cringed at the anger and hostility in his voice. "You teachers are always saying how important college is, but now you're wrecking my chance to get picked by a college scout!"

"You should have thought of that earlier," the coach said calmly.

"The Blub is a boy of very little brain," Keith murmured. "*Thought* isn't his department!"

"Academic probation is not the end of the world," the coach said. "It isn't permanent. Bring up your grades, and you're back on the team—provided we get the other problem resolved."

"It could take months to bring up my grades!" Tad protested. "What if football season is over by then? I'll lose my chance at a college scholarship!

I'll lose my chance to go to college at all!"

"His best bet's an academic scholarship," Keith said knowingly to the math team boy. "I bet he wins one in nuclear physics."

"No way," said the math team boy. "Quantum mechanics."

Claire whirled on them. "Can't you see this is serious?"

Ken caught a glimpse of a beefy arm lashing out to sweep a stack of books off the coach's desk. The books cascaded to the floor in a series of crashes.

"What am I supposed to do now?" Tad yelled, angry tears in his voice, which was loud enough to carry out into the gym. "You're destroying my future! You're destroying my whole life!"

Nobody in the gym was practicing layups anymore.

"Tad, take a minute and calm yourself down. Sit down here—"

A chair flew across the room and smashed into the wall near the door. Ken decided it was time to get involved. He peered around the door. "Uh, Coach? Is there anything—"

"I don't want to calm myself down!" Tad screamed, oblivious to his teammate's presence. "I want to play football! All I ever wanted was to

113

play football!" He plucked a trophy from the corner of the desk and hurled it across the room. Ken ducked as it slammed into the wall over his head.

Coach Schultz reached for Tad's arm, but the big desk was between them, and the large boy threw off his hands. In a rage he reached for a hockey puck and grasped it like a Frisbee.

"Get down!" Ken yelled at Jessica and Amy, who'd edged into the room behind him. The coach grabbed at Tad's arm again and managed to wrest the hockey puck away from the boy.

Tad spiraled away from the teacher's desk. Ken dove for him, but Tad twisted out of his reach and Ken crashed into the wall. Tad grasped the edge of a small bookshelf and pulled it over, dashing its contents across the floor. Ken lunged forward to tackle Tad with Todd, Claire, and Bryce piling on top of the linebacker from the other direction.

When the bell rang a few minutes later, Tad was leaving for the front office, escorted by Coach Schultz, and Ken and the rest of his classmates hadn't even had time to change and shower. Ken's muscles were already aching from being thrown against the wall, but he wasn't really hurt. He stood for a moment, reviewing

114

what had happened and surveying the destruction in the football coach's office.

Football is too aggressive and violent.

He remembered seeing Freeverse's words on his computer screen. At the time he'd been positive that she was wrong—that nobody who really understood the game would think so. But right now he didn't know. For once he was glad Freeverse went to a different school. At least she hadn't been there to witness Tad's outburst.

Chapter 8

"Poor guy," Elizabeth said to no one in particular. She was staring at the gym door after Tad, who'd just left with Coach Schultz for the principal's office.

"That's for sure," answered a familiar voice.

She turned to see Todd standing beside her.

"Isn't this whole business terrible?" he asked, his voice a little stilted. He was also looking at the door rather than at her, but Elizabeth knew from his forlorn profile that he wanted to make up as much as she suddenly did.

She nodded. "It is terrible," she said softly, feeling her anger sliding away. She turned to him with a weak smile, knowing the most terrible part of the whole situation was feeling so far away from Todd. The anger she'd been harboring against him slowly began to slip away, and she put her arm through his.

Todd returned her smile. "It's a shame how somebody can say or do some idiot thing in the heat of the moment and screw things up so badly."

"If Tad had just ignored Nicky's comment before the game," Elizabeth began, "instead of turning into a wild animal—"

Todd jerked his arm away. "Tad?" he exclaimed. "I was talking about Nicky!"

Elizabeth noticed Jessica and Lila watching them and made an effort to modulate her voice. "Nicky was out of line, but that doesn't excuse—"

"A minute ago you sounded sympathetic to Tad!" Todd protested, his eyes accusing her.

"I am sympathetic!" Elizabeth countered. "I feel sorry for him because he's dug himself into such a deep hole that he can't get out."

Todd was yelling now, and a larger group of students was taking notice. "If Blubber dug the hole, then Nicky handed him the shovel! And now Blubber's whole future is history!"

"You can't blame Nicky for Tad's future," Elizabeth protested. "Tad's situation is his own fault, for using his fists instead of his brain!"

"Of the two, I'd say his fists are the more potent tool," Keith put in.

Elizabeth and Todd whirled on him. "Mind your own business!" they said in unison.

Todd stared at her intently. "How would you feel if all you did was defend yourself, and suddenly the doors to your future were slammed in your face because of it?"

"Right on!" yelled Bryce.

"He was defending himself against hot air!" Elizabeth cried, trying to ignore the audience. "And he slammed those doors himself."

Justin gave her a thumbs-up. "She's got you there, El Jocko," he called to Todd.

Todd grabbed Elizabeth's arm and pulled her to a more isolated spot near the locker-room doors. "Liz, what is with you?" he demanded through clenched teeth. His voice was quiet but tight with repressed anger. "I don't understand how you can be so cold! You're always soapboxing about how important college is. Now Tad might never be able to go, and you're acting like there's some sort of justice to that!"

"What does he need college for anyhow if all he wanted to do there was play football?" Elizabeth asked.

"Elizabeth!" Todd cried, loud enough so that

heads turned all over the gym. "You're being cruel and unreasonable!"

"You're the one who's blindly taking the jock side in everything, no matter how idiotic it may be!"

"In case you haven't noticed," Todd said, "I *am* an athlete! If you can't be there for your friends, who can you be there for?"

She glared up at him. "I thought *I* was your friend!"

"So did I!" Todd countered. "When are you going to start acting like it?"

On Wednesday morning Olivia was walking through the Sweet Valley High parking lot with Elizabeth, wishing she were going anywhere but to school.

"I am so sick of this war of the cliques," Olivia said. "Do you really think there's something the *Oracle* can do to keep everyone from scratching each other's eyes out?"

"I honestly don't know," Elizabeth said. "But we've got to try. That's why Mr. Collins called the staff meeting for this morning. Maybe with some careful, sensitive coverage of the issues—"

"Speaking of issues, what do you make of that?" Olivia asked, pointing. The girls stopped to watch the scene that was unfolding in front of them.

The front steps of the school were carpeted with sitting students, and more were arriving every moment. Many of the protesters wore tie-dyed T-shirts, leather, fringes, or plaid flannel. Jan sprawled on the top step, hanging on to one end of a banner that read, No More Competitive Sports! Justin's sign said, Replace Football with Hacky Sack! He and many of the others were holding the embroidered beanbag balls they used for Hacky Sack, a low-key game that was a favorite activity on the smoking ramp.

As Olivia and Elizabeth watched, two of their friends—punker Dana Larson and artist DeeDee Gordon—ran past them from the parking lot and found seats on the steps.

"Yo! Davidson and Wakefield!" called Keith, who stood on the edge of the group, lounging against a pillar and wearing a guitar on a strap around his neck. "Join our antijock sit-in!" he yelled.

"Not Wakefield, man!" called a sophomore boy from the steps, wearing a Beavis and Butt-head T-shirt. "She's dating a prepped-out basketball player!"

"Be cool," Keith urged. He looked at Elizabeth. "I heard you tell off Todd in gym class Monday. That was excellent!"

Elizabeth shifted uncomfortably. Olivia knew she was still feeling hurt and angry about the things Todd had said to her. Instead of replying, Elizabeth steeled her shoulders and pulled out her reporter's notebook. Olivia admired her for having the presence of mind to think about the school newspaper in the midst of everything. "Why do you want to ban team sports?" Elizabeth asked the group.

"Jocks are thugs!" Jan hollered from the top step.

"The school shouldn't be supporting rivalry and competition," Justin said more reasonably. "Why don't we emphasize activities that encourage students to work together instead of against each other?"

"We have those too," Ken Matthews said, walking up behind Olivia and Elizabeth. "There's the marching band, the choir, school plays, the art club—"

DeeDee stood up, hands on her hips. "Do you know how the art club's budget compares to the cheerleading squad's?" she asked. "And when was the last time anyone won a trophy or a letter jacket for being in a school play?"

"Team sports do encourage students to work together!" Ken said. "And they bring students together as spectators too."

"They bring students at our school together," Olivia said thoughtfully, thinking about Quarter, "but only because they pit one school against another. Why should students at, say, El Carro be our enemies?"

"Right on!" Keith yelled. The steps were filling up fast—with new arrivals taking seats on the lawn in front of the building. Ken shook his head and walked away. Keith began strumming on the guitar. Olivia recognized the tune of John Lennon's "Imagine."

Elizabeth touched Olivia's shoulder. "Come on," she urged her friend. "We've got an *Oracle* meeting to go to."

"Aren't you two planning to sit in with us?" Justin asked over the sound of Keith's music.

"No," Elizabeth said slowly. "I'm against Tad's violent behavior, and I agree that the school emphasizes sports unfairly over other activities—"

"So what's your problem?" Jan asked.

"I can't agree with abolishing competitive sports altogether," Elizabeth replied. "I'm not interested in being on an athletic team, but I think they have a place at our school just as much as the school newspaper or the chess club does."

Keith stopped strumming. "What about you, Olivia?" he called out. "I know you agree with us!"

Olivia took a deep breath. "I guess I do," she announced, just now realizing it was true. "But I'm on the newspaper staff. I can't cover this controversy if I'm involved in it."

"Wimp!" Jan hollered from the top step.

"Be mellow," Keith called up to Jan. "*Nonviolent* protest, remember? Make love, not war!"

Elizabeth and Olivia threaded their way through sitting students as they climbed the steps. "Do you think their protest will do any good?" Elizabeth asked after they were inside the building.

"I wish," Olivia said hopelessly. "But it's not going to happen. Not in a million years! Face it—competitive sports are here to stay. They bring in revenue, build school spirit, get publicity for Sweet Valley High—"

"Those aren't bad things," Elizabeth pointed out as they walked through the bustling hallway.

Olivia shrugged. "Maybe not. But I've always thought it unfair that sports take precedence over everything else. For instance, when was the last time classes were canceled so we could all attend a pep rally to cheer on the band before it marched in a parade or something?"

"Never," Elizabeth admitted.

"Exactly. But we do it for football games all the time!"

"And DeeDee was right about budgets," Elizabeth agreed. "Groups like the art club get no money at all from the school. Even the *Oracle* staff had to wash cars to raise money for that special issue last month!"

"I'm sick and tired of it," Olivia admitted. "I really was tempted to join them."

"Why didn't you?" Elizabeth asked. "I mean, I heard what you said about journalist objectivity, and I respect it. But you're the arts editor, not the news editor. Nobody would fault you for getting involved if you feel strongly about it."

"It's more than that," Olivia said. "I don't know. Some of those people are my friends. I even dress like a lot of them," she added, looking down at her loose embroidered gauze dress and fringed vest.

"But you don't really *feel* like one of them," Elizabeth guessed, staring intently into her eyes.

"How can you tell?"

"I think you're kind of in the same boat as me," Elizabeth said, continuing to walk down the hall. "Not fitting neatly into any one category."

Olivia let out a short laugh. "Yeah, you're right about that," she said. "I dress like the hippies. I'm into art, but I have a lot of other interests too. I get good grades, but not in every

124

subject like the brains—" She looked over at Elizabeth. "No offense, Liz. You're smart in everything, but I don't think of you as part of that crowd exactly either."

"It's OK," Elizabeth said. "I know exactly what you mean."

"I've got plenty of pals," Olivia said. "But they're all across the board—artists, jocks, brains, punkers. Where is it written that all your friends have to be part of one clique?"

"It's not," Elizabeth said. "I've got friends all across the board too."

"Yes, you do," Olivia said. "Besides Winston, you're the only person I know who seems to become part of the in crowd for every crowd you hang with. I wish I could be like that too."

"I think most of your friends would say the same thing about you," Elizabeth assured her.

Olivia shook her head sadly. "No, they wouldn't. The difference between you and me is that you seem to fit in with *all* the groups and I fit in with none of them."

Elizabeth stopped, staring at her friend again. "Do you really see it that way?"

"Absolutely!" Olivia cried. "I'm too different from everybody else! Sometimes I think I'll always be on the outside."

"There's nothing wrong with being different," Elizabeth said staunchly, stopping at the door to the *Oracle* office. "I've always admired your originality."

Olivia smiled gratefully, but she felt drained and depressed. "Thanks, but sometimes I think it would be a whole lot easier if I were more like everyone else."

A few hours later Elizabeth was sitting at a lunch table with Enid and Maria Slater. At the next table Jessica was flirting alternately with Bryce and Danny while Lila watched with her usual bored expression and Ken, Claire, and Bruce joked with them from across the table. But Elizabeth was too caught up in the newspaper's new project to pay much attention to them.

"The theme of the special *Oracle* issue will be 'In Each Other's Shoes,'" Elizabeth explained to her friends. "We're trying to use every section of the paper to promote understanding among all the different groups of kids at school."

"It sounds awesome," Enid agreed. "And not a moment too soon. When's it coming out?"

"Not until a week from Friday. There's too much to do to get it together."

"I've never seen a dessert this color," Maria

complained, raising her spoon so they could see the grayish mass that glopped off it. "What do you think it's supposed to be?"

Enid wrinkled her nose. "Tapioca, I think."

"Gray tapioca?" Maria asked. "That should be illegal!"

All three girls turned as a tray clattered into the vacant spot on the adjacent table next to Ken. Elizabeth froze. The hands on the tray were Todd's. They had been avoiding each other since their argument after gym class Monday afternoon. He noticed her at the same moment as she saw him. Todd quickly looked away.

"Uh, I think I see Winston waving at me," he muttered. He gathered up his tray and hurried away to the other side of the room.

Jessica and her companions turned to stare curiously at Elizabeth for a moment. She bit her lip and gazed at her tray.

"As I was saying," Jessica began loudly, "what happened to Blubber was totally unfair. We need to do something to help get him back at school and back on the team!"

"I'm all for that!" Danny agreed.

"We have to show the riffraff who's really in charge of this school," Bruce called out, as if it were a challenge.

127

"I believe Principal Cooper is in charge," Maria put in from Elizabeth's table. "And he's called for an end to the violence and vandalism—though I know that destructive actions are the only thing some people understand." She glared at them evenly.

"Blubber wouldn't have had to use destructive actions if Nicky hadn't used destructive words first," Bryce said.

"That is so true, Bryce," said Jessica, flashing him a dazzling smile. "You really have a way of cutting to the point!"

"Yes, it is true," Danny said, slitting his eyes at Bryce. Then he turned to Jessica. "And those same people who are arguing against violence staged that bonehead protest in front of the school this morning!"

Jessica placed a hand on his shoulder. "That is an excellent point, Danny. Very insightful!"

"It was a peaceful protest!" Elizabeth argued.

Bruce shrugged. "No thanks to those radicals," he said. "Do you know how easily that mob could have gotten out of hand? Whose fault would that have been?"

"Whose fault is this gray tapioca?" Claire interrupted. "This stuff is disgusting!"

"Chemical warfare," Maria replied.

"Face it, Liz," Jessica said. "It's not Blubber's fault he got thrown off the team. And it's not us jocks who are keeping this war alive. Those hippies didn't have to have their little sit-in today! They're just trying to get people riled up!"

Enid rolled her eyes. "As if people could be any more riled up than they are now—"

A blast from the loudspeakers split the room apart, vibrating the already charged atmosphere like thunder. Hard-core punk music roared into the cafeteria. Elizabeth clapped her hands over her ears.

"What the heck is that?" Bruce was obviously yelling, but Elizabeth made out his words only by reading his lips. At the far end of the room she caught a glimpse of Dana giving Jan a thumbs-up sign.

After a minute the music died abruptly, and Principal Cooper's amplified voice blared through the school, assuring the students that those who had sabotaged the loudspeaker system would be caught and punished.

"Give 'em the chair!" Bruce cried.

"That's constructive," Ken said.

"What's this, Matthews, are you siding with the hippies and burnouts?" Bruce taunted. "Ready to

129

trade in your football for a Hacky Sack beanbag?"

"No way, man!" Ken said. "I just wish we could all leave each other alone and do our own thing—"

His voice trailed off. Elizabeth followed his gaze and saw a carroty head of hair rising above a group of seated students. The boy, a sophomore, was in her gym class, but Elizabeth didn't know him personally except that he was on the math team and was considered brilliant. From this distance she couldn't make out his words, but he seemed to be making some sort of speech.

One of Todd's basketball teammates stood up and made an obscene gesture at him. Jan was scowling at the math team boy too, Elizabeth saw. The lanky, vacant-eyed girl yelled something back at him, though Elizabeth still couldn't hear what they were saying. The boy clenched his fists at his sides and screamed at Jan. The din in the cafeteria was quieting as people turned to watch.

"Have some gray matter, brainiac!" hollered a girl's voice above the fray. A bomb of tapioca exploded in the boy's face, plastering his thick glasses.

"Oh, yeah?" yelled somebody else. "How

about some milk to go with that!" Elizabeth glimpsed the basketball player's white blond hair disappear under a shower of chocolate milk. Within moments mashed potatoes, peas, and gravy were flying through the air throughout the room.

"My hair!" Jessica cried, shielding it with a notebook. Lila was awkwardly crawling under the table. She looked about as inelegant as Elizabeth had ever seen her.

"Let's get out of here!" Elizabeth screamed toward Enid and Maria. Enid had cottage cheese on her forehead. Elizabeth jumped up, skidded on some overcooked spinach, and would have fallen if Maria hadn't grabbed her arm.

"We can leave the room, but there's no getting away from it all," she heard Ken say as she brushed past him. Something in his voice disturbed her. He sounded as lost and hopeless as Olivia had when she'd talked about not fitting in anywhere.

Elizabeth was beginning to feel lost as well. Ken had been her friend for as long as she could remember; she'd even dated him for a time. And she was still in love with Todd despite being so mad at him. But now they were on opposite sides of the Clique Wars, and as Ken had said, there was no getting away from it all.

"*Getting away is bliss,*" Olivia typed into the laptop computer she'd borrowed from her father. She dipped her toe in the cool water of Secca Lake and relished her temporary respite from the upheaval and hard feelings at school.

"*There was a major food fight at lunch today,*" she continued her electronic journal entry, "*and a prank with the public-address system, and a sit-in in front of the school. So much dissension, so much anger. I'd much rather sit here after a long, lovely hike in the woods and watch the sun setting over the lake.*"

The hike in the woods had been a virtual one, but she'd been with Quarter, so it had been more fun than any real-world hike with anybody else. They'd left the chat room and gone off-line a few minutes earlier, but her lakeside perch was so peaceful that Olivia couldn't bring herself to pack up the computer and go home—at least until the sun went down. So here she was, sitting on a rock on the edge of the lake, watching flashes of gold and pink rippling across its surface as she typed.

"*The hike was awesome,*" she wrote. "*Quarter described a little clump of violets and the bright*

132

green moss that grows near the roots of trees. He knew the names of the different kinds of rocks when I described the ones here by the lake, and when I asked how he knew, he said science was his favorite subject."

That had surprised her. She'd pegged him as an arts-and-humanities type. "Haven't you ever heard of physics for poets?" Quarter had joked.

"He's not an intellectual, but he's intelligent," she punched into the laptop, *"with a sense of humor and a sense of fun."*

At the end of their virtual hike they'd had a picnic on a ridge overlooking a river. Olivia had sketched the scene while Quarter fed her deviled eggs and made wacky jokes about picnics and ants.

"Have I finally found someone who understands me?" she wrote. *"Is my soul mate walking the halls of El Carro High School?"* She stared out over the sunset-colored lake and asked the next question aloud: "And can I actually be falling in love—with a guy I've never met?"

Chapter 9

"I don't understand it," Elizabeth said as she ripped apart a head of lettuce that night in the Wakefield family's Spanish-tiled kitchen. Jessica wondered whose face her sister was imagining on that leafy green head. "Why can't everybody at school learn to work and play well together? Kindergartners do it!"

"Because the burnouts and the hippie-radical freaks won't let us!" Jessica answered. She tossed a handful of forks onto the table.

"Setting the table means putting the flatware at every place, not in a clump in the middle," Elizabeth reminded her.

"Whatever," Jessica replied, rolling her eyes. Elizabeth, she thought, was way too uptight about things like setting the table. What did it matter, as long as there were enough forks for everyone? "I suppose you think this whole situation is the jocks' fault?"

"The fight at the football game definitely was," Elizabeth said. "But all sides are contributing to keeping the fight going now."

"That isn't true!" Jessica cried. "The jocks are perfectly content to stop fighting and go back to the way things have always been. It's the other groups who are trying to change everything!"

"Maybe some things need to be changed!"

"But everybody used to get along fine," Jessica protested. "Or at least they stayed out of each other's way."

"As far as the jocks are concerned, everybody getting along means that everyone who's not on a varsity team has to sit by and watch the athletes get all the recognition and all the consideration."

Jessica shrugged, holding a glass in each hand. "It works for me."

"Because you actually agree with the jock jerks? Or because you're getting such a kick out of stringing along two football players?"

"In case you haven't noticed," Jessica said acidly, "I'm one of the 'jock jerks.' I am a cheerleader, after all."

"I didn't say all jocks were jerks. I just meant the ones who advocate violence and think they're better than everyone else!"

"Maybe they really are better than everyone else!"

"You can't really believe that!" Elizabeth said. "Why can't we all coexist as equals?"

"You sound like you ate the Declaration of Independence."

"I'm serious, Jessica! Why can't everyone just get along?"

"Right!" Jessica scoffed. "And replace football with Hacky Sack!"

"You know I didn't mean—" Elizabeth tried to break in, but Jessica cut her off.

"I can see it now," Jessica exclaimed. "I could wear a plaid flannel cheerleading uniform and granola-eater sandals, and I'd lead the squad as we cheer on the mighty Hacky Sack team to victory! As if any of those burnouts could air out their cloudy little minds long enough to figure out who won!"

"I didn't say—"

"My pom-poms would smell like clove smoke forever," Jessica continued, remembering Justin blowing smoke rings on the ramp the week before. "I know! Let's cheer at chess club tournaments too!"

"Why not?" Elizabeth asked, her hands on her hips. "Chess players practice just as hard as football players. Why shouldn't they get noticed too?"

Jessica hooted. "Get a clue, Liz. They're nerds! Like that scrawny little redheaded twit who started the food fight today. I had to wash my hair three times this afternoon to get the mashed potatoes out!"

"Getting a face full of tapioca doesn't exactly qualify him as the aggressor," Elizabeth said. "I blame the fight on whoever *fired* the first tapioca."

"And I suppose you think it was a jock."

"How should I know if it was a jock?" Elizabeth asked. "As far as I can tell, nobody's sure who started it."

"I bet it was either a punker or a burnout," Jessica guessed. "And when the jocks find out which group it was, we'll get even with the freakazoids. Wait and see!"

Elizabeth grabbed her arm. "That's just my point! I know we've always had cliques at school. But they've never been this totally important before. Why do we have to decide whether it was a punker or a burnout? Whatever happened to individuals?"

Jessica sighed. "That's what a clique is—a group of individuals! I don't know why I'm even bothering to explain it to you. You couldn't possibly understand what's going on."

"What's that supposed to mean?"

"How can someone like you have a clue about the importance of fitting in with a group of people who have the same interests and values?" Jessica asked, tossing a stack of napkins onto the table. "You don't fit in with anyone."

"That's not fair," Elizabeth objected, a wounded-animal look in her eyes. "I have plenty of friends!"

Jessica shook her head. "Enid is too much of a nerd to be part of any group," she said. "Though I guess you'd call her a brain. Maria Slater's got better options, but she's too shortsighted to see it, so she hangs with the brains too."

"What's wrong with that?" Elizabeth asked.

Jessica continued speaking, counting on her fingers as she ran through a mental list of her sister's friends. "Dana's a punker. Olivia's a hippie. Weird city! Did you see that dress she was wearing today? It was so twenty years ago!"

"I like the way Olivia dresses!" Elizabeth protested. "She has real style—"

"Then there's Maria Santelli. She's your

friend too. But she's a cheerleader, so she counts as a jock," Jessica continued her tally. When Olivia had described Elizabeth's friends as diverse, she'd made it sound like a compliment. Jessica spoke as if it were a crime. "Winston's a dweeb, even if he does hang out with jocks," she continued. "DeeDee's a flaky artist. Which makes Elizabeth—"

"*Just me!*" Elizabeth concluded, her voice raised in exasperation. "Why do I need a label to have an identity?"

Jessica sighed. "As I said, you just don't have a clue."

"I never had a clue about poetry until you started explaining how to read it," Ken typed into his computer Thursday night as he and Freeverse carried on another conversation in a private chat room.

"It's not your fault," Freeverse replied. *"So many high-school teachers are lousy at teaching poetry."*

"Maybe I'm just lousy at understanding it," he admitted.

"I doubt that," Freeverse said. *"My English teacher is fantastic, but I know he's an exception. A lot of teachers spend so much time drilling you*

on rhyme and meter that they never get around to the self-expression part."

"Actually my English teacher is great," Ken admitted, thinking of Mr. Collins's patient explanations and encouragement. *"I'm the one who's hopeless! Why don't they write it like people talk?"*

"Why don't you try writing some yourself?" Freeverse suggested.

Ken rolled his eyes at the computer screen. *"Sure, and for my next trick I'll win the Nobel Prize for Literature."*

"I'm serious!" she said. *"It's not as hard as it sounds. I'll teach you."*

"You're a brave woman," he typed in. *"I guess I'm game if you are. But remember that you're doing this at your own risk!"*

Ken couldn't believe he was agreeing to write a poem—and for a girl he knew only via modem. But in another way, he reflected, he knew Freeverse better than any girl he'd ever dated, including Jessica. He'd loved Jessica, but now he realized that their conversations had all been on the surface, about school or movies or football or food. He could gossip with Jessica or make out with her. But he could never talk freely with Jessica about absolutely any crazy thought that flitted through his brain. He could never try to make himself into something so different from what his friends knew him as.

Freeverse was the only person who gave him the freedom to say whatever was on his mind—and who supported him in dredging up thoughts he hadn't even known were there.

"First think about something you like a lot," Freeverse instructed, beginning the poetry lesson. *"Besides electronic chatting!"* she added with a smile. *":)"*

Without thinking, Ken typed, *"Football,"* but he erased the word without sending it to her. *"The beach,"* he wrote instead, seizing on their earlier conversations.

"What do you like about the beach?"

"All the stuff we've talked about before," he responded with a shrug. *"Seagulls, waves, sand."*

"That's a good start," Freeverse told him. *"Now take any of those words, visualize it, and make a sentence about it."*

"I don't know, Free," Ken said, skeptical. *"I'm rotten at this kind of thing."*

"Don't worry about writing poetry. Just give me a sentence in plain old everyday English—concrete terms are best," she urged. *"No one will hear it but you and me."*

"Remember, I warned you!" he typed. *"Here goes: 'Seagulls fly in the sky.'"*

"Good! That wasn't so hard, was it?" Freeverse asked. "Now let's work with that, make it more descriptive."

"Come again?"

"For instance, look at the verb fly," she directed. "It's OK, but it's not as vivid as it could be."

"But seagulls do fly!"

"Sure, they do. Most birds fly. What makes this flight different? Strong verbs are one of the most important tools of a writer."

"How else can you say that seagulls fly?" he asked, not sure what she was asking of him.

"How do they fly?" she asked. "I don't mean the process; I mean, what does it look like when they fly? Hold the image in your mind and then tell me. Describe their flight—describe their wings, maybe."

"They soar, I guess. They glide," Ken attempted, stumbling. "Their wings are kind of long and pointy, like white swords, slicing . . . I'm sorry. That's dorky. I told you I can't write."

"You're doing beautifully," Freeverse assured him. "Those are strong, vivid images—not the least bit dorky. What about the sky? What does it look like?"

"It's got puffy clouds," Ken decided quickly.

"Compare them to something."

"*Cotton candy,*" he said, beginning to be intrigued with the wordplay Freeverse was guiding him through.

"*Now give me back the new-and-improved sentence.*"

"*Uh, how about this: 'Seagulls slice through cotton candy clouds.'*"

"*Now you're writing poetry! A line of it at least.*"

Ken felt his eyebrows shoot up. "*Really?*"

"*Sure. You even put some alliteration in there.*"

"*I didn't mean to!*" he assured her. "*Seriously, doesn't that have something to do with the way the words sound?*"

"*It does,*" said her words on his screen. "*It's a repetition of the opening consonant sounds: 'cotton candy clouds.'*"

"*I can't take credit. I didn't even know I was putting it there!*"

"*You might not have known consciously,*" said Freeverse, "*but you knew instinctively that it sounded good. You're a natural! See? I knew you could write!*"

"*This isn't like learning to write,*" Ken keyed in slowly, shaking his head in amazement. He felt as if he was beginning to unearth things about himself that he'd never known before—though he wasn't sure exactly what those things were. *"It's more like learning a whole new way of looking at things!"*

"Which is exactly what writing is!"

Ken knew, objectively, that the line of poetry he'd just written wasn't a particularly good one. But he'd written it, and for a few minutes he'd had a glimpse of how a real writer might go about crafting the perfect image. It gave him almost as much of a thrill as rushing for a first down. *"English class was never like this!"* he typed. He grinned and then added a grin for Freeverse's benefit: *":)"*

"You're an awesome student!" she typed.

Ken stared at the words on his screen, marveling as always at how a girl could sit at a computer in El Carro and type words that showed up on his computer in Sweet Valley. But he knew they were connected by more than a phone line. She'd called him an awesome student and a natural writer. He wondered what else Freeverse saw him as. Did she see him as a boyfriend?

For that matter, did he see her as a girlfriend, like Jessica had been? One thing was for sure—Freeverse had quickly become very important to him. Almost as if he were in love with her.

"No way!" he said aloud. "I've never even met her!" He wondered what a sensitive, artistic girl like Freeverse would think of him if they did meet. He was the kind of guy she'd be fed up with in about two seconds, he decided ruefully. One of those violent, aggressive jocks. A dumb jock. One of the "cleat clique," as he'd heard Keith Wagner say.

"Who knows?" she keyed in. *"Maybe you'll now go off to college and major in English and then grow up to become the poet laureate!"*

"LOL," he said. *"Don't hold your breath!"*

"Speaking of college, have you decided where you're going?" Freeverse asked.

"Not really," Ken replied. *"I've thought about a few places: UCLA or Sweet Valley University, or maybe Central California State."*

"CCS has a top-rated language program," she told him.

Ken grimaced. He'd been considering CCS for its top-rated football program and famous coach. But he wasn't about to say so to Freeverse. *"Let's go somewhere!"* he typed instead to change the subject.

"What did you have in mind?"

"I missed a chance to go to Snow Mountain

145

with some friends this year," Ken told her, thinking about a spring-break trip that Todd had gone on with Winston, both twins, and a dozen other Sweet Valley High students. *"Why don't we do a virtual trip to the Rocky Mountains to make up for it!"*

"Cool!" Freeverse replied. *"I was at Snow Mountain once, and it was beautiful. But let's find a cozy little cybercabin away from all the tourists instead of staying at the lodge."*

"You read my mind."

"So where are we?" she asked.

"It's evening, and a steady snow is falling outside the windows of our log cabin."

"The moon is bathing the woods outside in a soft, milky light," Freeverse continued. As always her words on his computer monitor brought pictures to Ken's mind.

"It's beginning to feel chilly inside the cabin," he said.

"Yes, but we've got this beautiful, wall-size fireplace made of rustic stone, cut from the side of the mountain. Unfortunately I've always been clueless about lighting fires."

"No problem," Ken said. *"I'm a regular pyro pro. Pick up some of that kindling and listen carefully, Freeverse. Now it's my turn to be the teacher."*

❖   ❖   ❖

146

A fire crackled on the stone hearth, casting a warm glow over Olivia's features and the features of the blond boy who sat beside her in the log cabin. She turned her head to gaze out the window at the snow that fell silently through stark black trees. *"It looks like a Robert Frost poem,"* she typed to Quarter.

For a moment the scene unfolding on Olivia's computer screen—and in her imagination—had seemed so real, she had to stop and remind herself that she was still sitting in her cluttered and utterly familiar bedroom.

"Was he any relation to Jack Frost?" Quarter asked. *"If so, I think he's responsible for the icing on the windows."*

"The fire's toasty," she told him, *"but just looking at frosted windows always makes me cold. I guess I'm too used to southern California."*

"I can help with that," Quarter said. *"Here. Can you feel me slipping my arm around your shoulders?"*

A warm tingle began in Olivia's shoulders and spread to her arms. *"Mmmm,"* she typed. *"I believe I can. You're wearing one of those thick, Irish fisherman's sweaters, right? The ivory-colored ones with a lot of texture?"*

"Sure," he replied. "That sounds about right. But your hand is still cold, so I'd better take it in mine, if that's all right with you."

"Yes, I'd like that," she keyed in, barely breathing. "Your hand is warm and strong, and your eyes are reflecting the orange glow of the fire." Suddenly she realized her scene was missing something. "Your eyes—what color are they? Would you describe them to me?"

"They're blue," he responded. "It's hard for me to describe my own eyes, but people tell me they're deep set, and they always comment on how dark the lashes are."

"They sound beautiful," Freeverse said.

"Now I'm gazing into your eyes. Fair's fair, Free. Describe them to me."

"My eyes are hazel," she said. "Sometimes they look greener and sometimes they look browner. Sometimes people even think they're blue."

"Ah, mysterious and unpredictable, just like you."

Olivia laughed with pleasure. No guy had ever said anything like that to her before.

"I know that your hair is blond," she said. "Tell me more about it."

"It's cut pretty short, but not short enough to keep a little bit of a wave from showing," Quarter responded.

148

"Mine is brown and curly, like I said before."
She frowned and decided she might as well be
honest with him. "And when I say curly, I really
mean curly. It's thick and wild and long and
frizzy. The kind of hair people refer to as 'a curly
mop' or a 'wild mane.'"

"Awesome!" Quarter replied. "Most of the
girls I know all have the same two or three hair-
styles. Yours sounds a lot more original!"

"I can't take any credit," she replied. "It's like
this naturally." She was surprised at his apparent
approval and then wondered why she was surprised. She always expected people to hate her
hair, but she usually discovered that she was the
only one who thought it was just too weird.

"I think I would like to run my fingers
through those wild, sexy curls," Quarter said.

"Only if I can touch your hair too," Olivia
typed back, mesmerized by his words and
shocked at her own courage.

"Your hair is gorgeous, Free. It feels like silk,
and all those curls are shimmering in the fire-
light. And now my hand strokes the side of your
face, and your skin is as soft as the petal of a
poppy."

"I can feel your fingertips," she typed, hardly
believing that this was happening. "They're

strong, but so gentle and relaxing. Now I'm touching your hair." She imagined his blond waves twining around her fingers. "It's lit white-gold by a moonbeam from the window, and I just brushed up against your ear, which is soft and warm and a little pink on top from spending too much time on the slopes today."

"I guess I forgot my sunblock again," Quarter admitted. "I've got a bit of sunburn on my shoulders too, but that's from the beach."

Olivia felt a rush of heat in her face and was glad he couldn't see her blushing. "I bet you have great shoulders," she guessed. "Tell me more about yourself."

"I guess my shoulders are kind of broad," he admitted. "At least people tell me so. I'm six-foot one, and I try to stay in good shape."

Olivia imagined him in her mind's eye—he was handsome and tall, with a great build. With a sinking heart she wondered what he was expecting her to look like. "There's not much to say about me," she typed. "I have totally ordinary looks—except for my crazy hair." She was embarrassed to be talking about looks, but she wanted to be honest with Quarter. It wouldn't be fair to mislead him into expecting a glamour girl.

"Ordinary? No way is there anything ordinary

about you, Freeverse! Besides, you're not allowed to pass any value judgments on yourself here."

"Is that a rule?"

"It is now. You can give only straight, objective description," he said. *"Paint a picture in my mind, like you're collecting images for a poem."*

Olivia smiled. *"Trapped by my own poetry lesson!"* she wrote ruefully. *"OK, I'll try. I'm five-foot five, and I have a totally average build. My face is a little on the round side, and I have wide-set eyes and kind of full lips."*

"What do you like about yourself?"

For a moment Olivia stared at the keyboard, stumped. All she and her girlfriends ever seemed to do was complain about what they *didn't* like about themselves.

Then she realized the answer was right in front of her. *"My hands,"* she said, surprised that she'd never thought of it before. *"I like my hands!"*

"Describe them to me."

"My fingers are kind of long, like they were meant to strum guitar strings or hold sketching pencils. The nails are short and stubby, which drives my mother crazy but is practical for painting and typing."

"I'm holding one of your hands now, and I'm

stroking it with my fingers," Quarter said. "The skin is soft—and despite what your mom says, I think your stubby fingernails are cute!"

"Did you notice the smear of green paint along the side of my right thumb?" Olivia asked with a laugh. "I never manage to get it all off after I've been painting."

"It's a lovely shade," he replied. "In fact, your hazel eyes are that exact same green right now. You artists are so good at being color coordinated!"

"I wouldn't want the stain on my hand to clash with my eyes," she said. "That would be a major fashion faux pas. :)"

"Now I'm running my hand up your arm," Quarter typed. "You're still a bit cold; I can feel the goose bumps. But you're warming up fast."

Olivia nodded. "Oh, yes!" she said aloud, sure that her temperature was shooting up like a geyser. She turned back to her keyboard. "Your hand feels wonderful on my arm. The warmth is spreading through my entire body."

"What about your lips?" he asked. "Are they warm too?"

"I'm not sure," she responded. "Maybe you should check and see."

"I'm leaning in toward your face, and you

152

look so beautiful right now as you gaze at me out of those big, hazel eyes."

"My fingers are entwined in the blond curls at the nape of your neck," she typed furiously, feeling as if she were writing a romance novel and living one at the same time. *"Your arms feel safe and warm around me."*

"Gently I press my lips against yours—"

Olivia closed her eyes and let out a slow, deep sigh. She couldn't believe this was happening to her. *"Your lips are like raspberries, as light as a whisper at first—"*

"And then you kiss me back, Freeverse, long and hard. And nothing has ever rocked me the way your kiss does."

"And we hold each other tightly as the flames cast orange-and-red tongues of light around the room," Olivia continued, breathless.

"And your body feels soft and warm, and fits perfectly against mine."

"Oh, man!" Ken said aloud to his empty room. He slumped in his desk chair, drained. The kiss he'd just shared with Freeverse had been incredible, even if it was only a virtual kiss. His pounding heart was sure real. So were his heavy breathing and the rush of electricity that still pulsed through his body.

The moment passed, and gradually Ken found he could breathe normally. He stared at the computer screen with no idea of what to do next. How did you follow up an on-line experience like that kiss?

Freeverse found an answer first. *"We've got to stop meeting like this!"* popped onto his screen after a minute of silence.

"And meet in real life?" Ken typed eagerly.

The moment he hit enter, Ken realized the enormity of what he'd done. He wanted to hold Freeverse, to kiss her for real. What if she didn't want to? Or worse, what if they met in person and the cyberspark had flickered out? He held his breath and waited.

Apparently Freeverse was feeling the same doubts. *"What if meeting in person means the end for us?"* she asked.

"I hope it doesn't, but it seems like we've got to find out sooner or later," he said. *"Do you really think it will be totally different, talking face-to-face?"*

"I don't know," she said. *"But I guess it's time to try. We have to know if this is for real."*

Chapter 10

"Is this for real?" Elizabeth said on Friday morning, holding out a letter that had been left in the in box at the *Oracle* office. She'd thought she was escaping the clique wars when she'd sought refuge in the newspaper office before homeroom. But they seemed to have followed her there.

Olivia looked up from the concert review on her computer monitor and took the page from Elizabeth's hand. "'Dear Editor,'" she read aloud. "'Blubber is a big fat thug. Now he's off the team and out of school, and I say good riddance. Dumb jocks and dumb blond fashion queens are ruining this school. Let's kick every last one of them out.'"

"Girlfriends, those grapes are way sour!" Maria Slater exclaimed from the next workstation. She was researching an article on getting along together she'd proposed for the arts section of the special issue. Maria wasn't a regular staff member, but she was an excellent writer who occasionally pitched in with a story. "What a phenomenally boneheaded letter! Who's the Shakespeare who composed it?"

"Naturally it's unsigned," Elizabeth said, "which means we can't run it in the newspaper."

"Somehow we'll find the courage to go on," Olivia joked.

Maria clicked off the Web site she'd been poring over, leaned back in her chair, and crossed her arms. "Did you hear about the jock sit-in going on in the gym right now?"

"I'm not sure I want to," said Olivia.

"They say it's in retaliation for the antijock protest on the front steps on Wednesday."

Elizabeth groaned. "I should probably go cover it for the *Oracle*," she said dismally.

Olivia gave her a sympathetic smile. "There's that journalistic enthusiasm that's an inspiration to us all!"

"I'm just so sick of this!" Elizabeth cried. "Why can't we all get over it and move on?"

"I wouldn't worry about rushing down to the gym, Liz," Maria said. "I ran into Penny and Tina Ayala there. Penny was scribbling furiously, and Tina was snapping photos."

"Thank goodness for our editor in chief," Olivia said, referring to Penny, who was a close friend of both Olivia and Elizabeth. "And with her sister there from the photography staff, it sounds like you're off the hook, Liz!"

"Speaking of sisters, did you notice if Jessica was involved in this thing?" Elizabeth asked Maria.

"Where football players congregate, the world's most dedicated cheerleader is never far away," Maria said. "She was making a speech into the microphone when I left the gym—something about school spirit and tonight's football game against Palisades High."

"It figures," Elizabeth said, shuffling through a stack of papers on Penny's desk, looking for the editorial she was supposed to copyedit.

"The jock sit-in wasn't getting violent, was it?" Olivia asked.

Maria shook her head. "It'll stay peaceful, as long as the opposition keeps its distance."

"I heard a bizarre rumor from Jessica this morning," Elizabeth said. "She claims that a

157

small private airplane is going to fly over the stadium during halftime at the Palisades game tonight and dump a load of flyers with antihippie slogans."

Maria hooted. "She's dreaming!"

"I wish I knew that for sure," Elizabeth said. "The jocks' side has Bruce's and Lila's millionaire resources behind it. Who knows how far they'd go?"

"Are you two planning on going to the game?" Olivia asked.

"Not me!" Maria said.

"I'm sitting this one out," Elizabeth said firmly. "I haven't missed a game all season, but I feel so out of place with those people lately."

Maria leaned forward and placed a hand on her shoulder. "Are you serious? I thought a lot of 'those people' were your friends!"

"They are," Elizabeth said. "Or they were. Now I don't even know if *Todd* is my friend anymore! We never actually broke up, but he's hardly said a word to me all week. I keep wondering if he thinks he should be dating a cheerleader or a girl on the track team or something."

"You're the one he loves!" Olivia said. "He'll come around. And so will the rest of your friends on the sports teams."

"Being the only nonathlete at a party never bothered me before," Elizabeth confided. "But lately, when I'm hanging out with Todd and Ken and the gang, I feel like there's a neon sign over my head flashing, Not a Jock. I'm not sure I fit in anymore."

Maria stood and began gathering her notebooks. "Elizabeth Wakefield, you are one of the most popular kids in this town! How can you be afraid of not fitting in?"

"Maybe I'm being silly and insecure," Elizabeth said. "If so, you can blame Jessica. We had a fight a couple nights ago, and you know how good she is at pushing my buttons!"

"That's what sisters are for," Maria said.

"I keep reminding myself of what I told her," Elizabeth said. "That I don't need a label in order to be who I am."

Maria gave her a thumbs-up signal. "Go, girl!"

"But I still have this vague sense that I'm—I don't know. *Weird*."

"I can relate," Olivia said with a laugh. "I even used to like feeling weird. Now I'm not so sure. You, on the other hand, are about as unweird as they come!"

"I second that!" Maria said. She checked her watch. "Well, I've got to get to homeroom early to interview Dana for this article I'm writing. So I'd better leave you two. See you at lunch!"

After Maria had gone, Olivia punched in a code to save her concert review, clicked the mouse to exit her word-processing program, and turned to Elizabeth. "You know, Liz," she said. "There is one place you can go where nobody cares about finding a label to classify you under."

Elizabeth turned toward her expectantly, and Olivia wondered if she should have kept her big mouth shut. What would practical, cautious Elizabeth say about her recent on-line obsession? But it was too late now. She'd already brought up the subject.

"On the Internet you can find people who couldn't care less whether you hang out with soccer players or with heavy-metal heads," Olivia said. "All you need to do is find a chat room with interesting people in it. Then start putting in your two cents. You wouldn't believe what a wonderful relationship you could find on-line!"

Elizabeth gazed at her curiously, a slow smile forming on her face. "Relationship? What relationship? Olivia, did you meet someone?"

Olivia giggled. "I never was good at poker faces. The truth is, I think I'm falling in love."

Elizabeth grabbed her arm, led her to an old, threadbare couch in a corner of the room, and plopped down beside her. "OK, spill it! I want to hear everything," she urged, her blue-green eyes twinkling.

"He's a junior like us, and he goes to El Carro High School," Olivia said.

"What's his name?"

"Quarter."

Elizabeth cocked an eyebrow. "Huh? Quarter of what?"

Olivia laughed. "Sorry. On my on-line service everyone goes by screen names. I'm Freeverse, and he's Quarter."

"Screen names? You mean you've only met this guy on your computer? You've never talked to him in person? You don't even know his real name?"

"Not yet," Olivia said.

"I guess it's safer to stay anonymous in case you meet someone who turns out to be a creep," Elizabeth acknowledged.

"Absolutely," Olivia agreed. "But don't worry. Quarter isn't a creep. It's amazing, Liz! We totally hit it off from the first time we talked."

"So tell me about him!"

"He's got a great sense of humor, and he's

161

warm and friendly and sensitive, and he likes the beach."

"You must know more than that!"

Olivia shrugged. "He's blond."

"Well, in that case, marry him quick—" Elizabeth joked.

"Liz, he understands me! I can say whatever crazy things I'm feeling, and he doesn't think I'm a space cadet. He's interested in poetry! And he always knows exactly the right thing to say."

"He sounds terrific," Elizabeth said. "But how can you know you're in love if you've never met him?"

"I admit that part's kind of odd," Olivia said. "But not for long. We have a date tomorrow afternoon!"

Elizabeth frowned. "A date? Just the two of you?"

"Of course it's just the two of us. Do you usually bring a chaperon along when you go out with Todd?"

"It's been so long since Todd and I have gone out that I barely remember," Elizabeth said dryly. "Olivia, are you sure it's safe to meet this guy by yourself?"

"Don't worry. I'm following all the safety protocols. I'm meeting him in broad daylight in an ice cream parlor in El Carro, where there should be plenty of people around."

"Why all the way over in El Carro?"

"It was my choice," Olivia said. "I don't want to risk running into anyone from school."

Elizabeth bit her lip. "I still don't know about this."

"It's sweet that you're worried, but I'll be fine."

"You could get into a lot of trouble, meeting a perfect stranger like that," Elizabeth warned. "What if you can't stand him, but he won't leave you alone afterward?"

"He doesn't have my name, address, or phone number," Olivia said. "How much of a pain in the neck can he be?"

"He could turn out to be a crackpot," Elizabeth said. "He could be downright dangerous!"

"You're paranoid," Olivia told her. "Personally I'm more worried that he'll turn out to be a loser. Or that he'll be perfect, but he won't like me once he sees me."

"Don't be so hard on yourself! You're talented, articulate, and attractive. If he has any sense at all, he'll be crazy about you!"

Olivia trembled with excitement. "That's the amazing thing, Liz. He says he already is crazy about me!"

163

"I'm glad for you," Elizabeth said. "And I don't mean to be a wet blanket. Just be careful!"

"I promise I will."

"I hope Quarter will turn out to be everything you expect and that you'll have a terrific date!" Elizabeth rolled her eyes. "At least you've *got* a date for this weekend, which is more than I can say for me and Todd."

The next afternoon Ken drummed his fingers on the edge of the marble-topped table at Izzy's Incredible Ice Cream shop in El Carro. He crossed his right leg over his left and then noticed that he was jiggling his foot so hard, the table was vibrating. He checked his watch for the third time in ten minutes. It was a few minutes before two o'clock. As usual he'd been sure to arrive early, just in case anything unexpected happened. But now the waiting was driving him wiggy.

He stared at the door, willing it to open. Freeverse should be walking in any minute now, he told himself. He imagined her wild, curly hair bouncing around her shoulders as she bounded into the room. He uncrossed his legs, thinking he would look less nervous if his foot wasn't jiggling wildly. What would Freeverse think when she met the real Quarter? And once they'd spoken in person, how long could he continue to keep her in the dark about who he really was?

If I wanted her to think I'm artsy, I could have gotten a clue about my clothes, he thought, realizing for the first time that his polo shirt and chinos were about as artsy as a Beach Boys hit. He hoped he wasn't about to blow his cover.

Freeverse would never know he was a jock from the way his team had played football the night before, he thought. Jessica's cheerleading squad could have suited up instead. At least they still had some spirit. *We blew it, pure and simple!*

All the guys had missed Tad on defense, of course, but something else was gone. Somebody—probably Bruce Patman, Ken guessed—had hired a plane to drop flyers over the stadium with the slogan, Nicky Had It Coming! But the intended audience never saw the taunt. The Sweet Valley stands were pitifully empty for the Palisades game. Only the bona fide jocks bothered to show up at all.

Ken wondered what Freeverse would say when she finally learned the truth—that Quarter wasn't a sensitive, free-spirited poet. That he was just another dumb jock. Would she be angry at him for hiding it? Would she be hurt? *Most likely,* he admitted to himself, *she'll drop me on the spot, as easy as fumbling a football.*

He glanced at his watch again and wished she would hurry. If he was about to get dumped, he didn't want to prolong his misery.

"What time is it, Lizzie?" Jessica asked, sprinting into the living room of the Wakefield house, where Elizabeth was lying on the sofa, reading.

Elizabeth closed her book and glanced at her watch. "It's nearly two o'clock. Why? Do you have a date?"

"Sort of. It's not until two-thirty, but I still have to fix my hair." She took in Elizabeth's forlorn expression and unfashionable sweatpants. "I take it you and Todd aren't seeing each other today?"

"Lately Todd doesn't notice anyone who's not in a team uniform!"

"Sorry," Jessica said sincerely. She didn't agree with her sister's view on the war of the cliques. But she hated to see Elizabeth unhappy, and she knew that wouldn't change until she and Todd were back together again, as boring and predictable as ever. "Speaking of clothes, are these white shorts too casual?"

"Too casual for what?" Elizabeth asked.

"For spending the afternoon cruising around in a convertible."

"They're fine," Elizabeth said. "Does that mean your date today is with Bryce?"

"Sort of," Jessica said again. "What about my top? Does the aqua color make my suntan look washed out?"

"The color is to die for on you, and you know it," Elizabeth told her. "But the top is a little bare, isn't it?"

Jessica shrugged. "If you've got it, flaunt it, right?"

Elizabeth rolled her eyes but let the remark pass. "So what's the big mystery? Is your date with Bryce or not?"

"Of course it is," Jessica said. "He's the one with the vintage convertible. But it's sort of a group thing."

"Are you and Bryce double dating with somebody?"

"It's more of a triple date," Jessica said.

"Three couples?"

"Three people," Jessica corrected, letting out an uncertain sigh. "Me and Bryce and Danny."

Elizabeth laughed. "You're going out on a date with two guys at the same time? Isn't that a little nutty?"

167

"Well, they both agreed to it," Jessica said. "I didn't exactly want to be alone with either one."

Elizabeth sat up. "Since when?"

"Since I'm fed up with hearing about nothing but football!" Jessica complained. "I swear, now that it's the jocks against everyone else at school, I can't even be seen having a conversation in the hallway with anyone who's not on a varsity team—except you."

"Why not?"

"It's considered high treason," Jessica explained, shaking her head incredulously. "It's a huge offense—if you believe Bruce Patman."

"I've never believed Bruce Patman!"

"And since we lost the Palisades game last night—no surprise there, without Blubber on defense—the jocks will be sticking together even more!"

"You sound like you're getting disillusioned with the whole situation," Elizabeth said.

Jessica cocked her head. "Not exactly. I mean, I still think Blubber got shafted, and I still think the burnouts, hippies, punks, and freaks are too weird for words. But can't I be a jock without having to hear about football every second of the day?"

"So then why are you going out with two football players?"

"Hello! Because they're cute," Jessica said. "And because when they're not talking about first downs and pass interceptions, they're constantly telling me how wonderful I am!"

Elizabeth laughed. "They both have it bad for you!"

"They think I'm the greatest thing since pigskin!" Jessica said. "And you know, I'm still not sure if that's a compliment."

Chapter 11

Olivia took a deep breath and glanced down at her outfit to make sure everything was in place. She'd changed her clothes four times before finally selecting a pair of batik-print sarong pants in royal purple with a matching loose vest over a simple white tank top. She knew it was an unusual outfit and that a lot of the guys at school—if they noticed her at all—would think it was wacky and New Age. But she was sure Quarter would see the beauty of the flowing lines and contrasting colors.

She pushed open the door of Izzy's Incredible Ice Cream. It was five minutes after two o'clock, but that wasn't too bad. Her parents were always telling her she was hopelessly disorganized.

Punctuality just wasn't a top concern for an artist. In this case it wasn't even her fault. She'd been driving around the block for at least five minutes, searching for a parking space.

Olivia scanned the room for the tall blond boy who would be Quarter. She caught sight of a boy's blond head at a marble-topped table in the corner. Then she blushed. Not only was the boy not Quarter—he was Ken Matthews.

"Just my luck!" she muttered. "What the heck is Ken doing in El Carro? So much for keeping a low profile."

Ken nodded to her, and she noticed his face was pink. *Probably sunburn from all those nasty football practices*, she thought. She returned his nod with a casual wave but didn't venture any closer. Quarter obviously hadn't arrived yet, and she didn't want to be talking to another guy when he finally showed. Besides, she couldn't imagine trying to explain to a jock like Ken exactly who she was meeting in an El Carro ice cream parlor and why.

She smoothed her wild dark curls, which had frizzed out more than usual because of the heat. She ordered a soda at the counter and carried it to an empty table near the window, trying to look nonchalant. After choosing the seat that gave her the best view of the door, Olivia pulled out her sketchbook to pass the time and settled in to wait for her mystery date.

Danny held open the door of the vintage convertible parked on the street in front of the Wakefields' split-level house. Jessica climbed in and slid across the seat until she was close to Bryce at the wheel. She could hardly believe she'd convinced both boys to go out with her today. But neither teammate had been willing to turn her down and risk leaving her alone with the other. Once Jessica was settled on the vinyl seat, Danny closed the door behind her and then vaulted over it to land beside her with a flourish.

"That was totally cool!" she said, bestowing a smile on him. Danny blushed with pleasure. "You are so athletic, Danny."

Bryce cleared his throat. "Where do you want to go, Jessica?" he asked.

"Oh, I don't know!" she said, throwing up her hands, which wasn't easy from her sandwiched position. "Does it really matter? In a majorly hot car like this one we'll look awesome wherever we go."

"We could just cruise around town a while and see what's shaking," Danny said, inching closer to Jessica on the seat.

"Or we could drive out to Secca Lake and enjoy the scenery," Bryce suggested.

"Let's stay in town," Jessica decided. "What good is riding in a convertible if there's nobody around to show off to?"

Danny beamed, and Bryce seemed disappointed that she'd taken Danny's recommendation over his. Jessica leaned on Bryce's shoulder as he pulled the car away from the curb. "You must know an awful lot about mechanical things to restore a classic old convertible so beautifully!" she gushed.

"I ran into Todd at the arcade this morning," Danny said quickly. "He was playing computer games like I was. But he seemed pretty down. Are he and your sister still—"

Jessica made a sour face. "Unfortunately," she said.

"But you've never approved of Liz dating Todd!" Bryce reminded her.

"I know I complain about Todd all the time," Jessica said. "Face it, for a major basketball star the guy is boring—even if he does drive a BMW!"

"Then what's the problem?"

"Life is simple for me when Liz is happy," Jessica said with a shrug. "When she's happy, it's

173

easier to borrow her clothes, get her to do the cooking when it's my turn, and make her help me with my homework."

"It sounds like a good deal if you can get it," Danny said, looking out as the shops of downtown Sweet Valley slid by. "Do you rent her out?"

"Lately *I* can't even get a lot of favors from Liz," Jessica complained. "So putting her up for rent is not an option. My twin has been positively postal ever since that O.K. Corral scene in the school gym, when she and Todd went at each other!"

"She's still siding with the burnouts over us?" Bryce asked. "What's up with that?"

"For someone who's supposed to be smart, my sister has zero common sense," Jessica said, shaking her head to make the sunlight glisten in her hair for the guys' benefit. She sighed. "But I still hate seeing her with those sad puppy dog eyes—like she was giving me at home a few minutes ago."

"I never thought a rivalry between cliques could break up Todd and Liz," Danny said. "They've always seemed so committed."

"Sometimes I think they ought to be committed," Jessica said.

"I bet this breakup doesn't last," Bryce predicted. "They're lost without each other. They'll kiss and make up sooner or later."

"I think you're right," Jessica agreed. "In a few more days they'll get nostalgic about all their dull, goody-two-shoes memories of all their dull, goody-two-shoes dates. And they'll get a clue."

"It doesn't even make sense that this clique thing created problems between them," Danny said. "Most of the jocks have always accepted Liz just fine!"

Jessica adopted a pained expression. "Yes, but my poor, deluded twin isn't sure she wants to be accepted by the jocks right now. We're not good enough for Elizabeth Wakefield, Girl Crusader."

"I suppose she'd rather share a clove cigarette and a game of Hacky Sack with Justin and Jan on the smoking ramp?" Danny asked.

"She'd run naked through the school cafeteria before she'd do that!" Jessica said with a laugh.

Bryce nodded thoughtfully. "Can I get a ticket for that event?"

"All I know," said Jessica, "is that this jock-versus-hippie-versus-whatever thing has gotten way out of hand if it can come between my sister, Mary Poppins, and her loyal, BMW-driving

175

slave. I wish they'd just get along with each other, you know?"

"Is that an anticonflict statement I'm hearing from Jessica 'Death to Freaks' Wakefield?" asked Bryce. "Have you joined the peace and free love crowd?"

Jessica sat back and crossed her arms in front of her aqua midriff top. "The same day I join the audiovisual club," she said archly.

Maybe Freeverse knows I lied to her about being a sensitive, artsy type, Ken told himself as he waited at the corner table at Izzy's Incredible Ice Cream. *That's why she hasn't shown up*.

Ken's thoughts rambled ahead of him as he idly watched Olivia Davidson drink a soda near the window. He wondered what the heck had brought her to El Carro. At the moment he hardly knew what had brought *him* there. It was forty minutes after two o'clock now; Freeverse was way late. Was she standing him up? *Why?* he asked himself. Had she learned that he played quarterback for the SVH football team—and that he'd hidden it from her? No, Ken decided. Freeverse couldn't possibly know that Quarter was really a jock in poet's clothing. If she was blowing off their date, it must be for a different reason.

He considered the possibilities. What if Freeverse had been lying about herself to him as well—or at least sidestepping any potential problems? What if she wasn't what she claimed to be either? She might even be more of a fake than "Quarter" was!

On the other hand, Freeverse might have a totally legitimate excuse for not meeting me here today as planned, he tried to convince himself. *A death in the family, an illness, some sort of crisis. Or maybe she just changed her mind about wanting to meet me. . . .*

Ken continued watching the door. Around three o'clock Olivia Davidson left the shop. But Ken stayed at his table a long time, even after it became clear that Freeverse was a no-show.

Finally he rose to his feet, pushing off from the marble tabletop with his hands. His eyes swept the bright, cheerful room once more, but Ken knew he wouldn't see a teenage girl with a mop of unruly brown curls. He felt utterly dejected. He sighed deeply and then trudged out the door, not sure if he could face his soul mate on-line ever again.

"Where to next?" Bryce asked a half hour later after they'd cruised by the beach in his convertible.

The weather was perfect for driving—a little bit warm but sunny, with the smell of the sea in the air and rows of palm trees swaying in the breeze. Jessica sat between two handsome, adoring guys—drinking mineral water, laughing, and gossiping. "Heard It Through the Grapevine" was cranking on the tape deck, and the warm wind streamed through her hair. "It doesn't get any better than this," she announced in parody of a television commercial.

"I've got it!" Danny cried. "Let's run by Blubber's house to see how he's doing. I sure missed him last night."

"We all missed him," Jessica agreed. "If he'd been playing in that game, everything would have been different! But are you sure he'll *want* to see us?"

Bryce glanced at her curiously. "Of course he will! Why wouldn't he?"

"I don't know. Maybe he'd be embarrassed about being on academic probation," Jessica suggested.

Bryce nodded. "Yeah, I can understand how it would be rough for him to hang out with three straight-A students like ourselves."

Danny laughed. "Does anyone have one of those flyers that rained down on the stadium?

The Blub would get a major kick out of seeing one—unless Zack brought one home from the game for him."

"Check the backseat," Bryce told them. "There ought to be a few back there."

As Bryce steered the car into the Johnsons' neighborhood Jessica climbed onto her knees and leaned over the backrest to root around for one of the Nicky Had It Coming! flyers.

"Here's one!" she cried, twisting back into her seat. "I bet Tad will feel better if he knows how much all his friends are supporting him in this."

"Supporting him?" Danny said. "We're practically tearing apart the whole school for him! He's gotta know we're with him, one hundred—"

"*What are those lights?*" Jessica called out sharply.

She pointed up ahead toward Tad's house. Flashes of red, white, and blue sparkled through the trees, and Jessica suddenly realized she'd been hearing a siren. As the convertible approached Tad's house she saw a rescue van parked in the driveway and two police cruisers by the curb.

"Oh, no!" Jessica breathed, her heart thudding to her feet. "What's going on here?"

Bryce jerked the convertible to a screeching

halt in front of the house next door. Jessica followed Danny's lead and jumped out of the car without bothering to open the door. She raced with her companions toward the Johnsons' driveway, where two emergency workers were toting a stretcher. A middle-aged woman ran alongside the workers, sobbing hysterically. Tad's brother, Zack, was right beside her. Jessica caught a glimpse of the person on the stretcher as it was loaded into the rescue squad. She felt the blood drain from her face.

"It's Blubber!" she said, tears welling in her eyes.

The rescue squad sped away, sirens wailing into the distance. Jessica, Danny, and Bryce ran to a police officer who stood in the driveway, writing something in a notebook.

"What happened, Officer?" Bryce asked, his face ashen.

The officer shook his head sadly. "The kid tried to take his own life."

Chapter 12

By late afternoon Olivia couldn't stand the suspense any longer. Biting her lip, she sat at her desk and logged onto her computer. The chat room was empty when she navigated her way into it except for one name: Quarter. Her heart skipped a beat.

"I was wondering if you'd be back," he said.

"You were?" she typed nervously. *"Quarter, I don't get it. Why here and not at the ice cream parlor?"*

"What do you mean? I was at the ice cream parlor. You're the one who stood me up!"

"But I was there!" she insisted. Olivia suddenly felt a stab of misgiving. Could she have been waiting at the wrong shop? That would

have been incredibly dumb of her, she reflected. But she'd done incredibly dumb things before. She took a deep breath before typing, *"We agreed on Izzy's at the El Carro Square shopping center, right?"*

"That's right," Quarter said. *"At two o'clock. And you never showed. I know, because I was there! I waited an hour and a half. Where were you?"*

"I was sitting at a table by the front window," she typed, frustrated, *"drinking a diet Coke and watching for you!"*

For a moment Quarter didn't reply. Then a single word appeared on Olivia's monitor: *"Olivia?"*

Olivia stared, startled at the sight of her real name. How could he know her name? Then her mouth dropped open as she visualized the scene at Izzy's that afternoon. Suddenly she felt queasy. *"Ken Matthews?"* she typed.

"Of course," she whispered, shocked. "Quarter for quarterback."

Her gentle El Carro poet was a Sweet Valley jock.

"What does it matter if he's a jock?" Elizabeth said aloud to Prince Albert, the Wakefield family's golden retriever. He had been standing at the side of the backyard pool, watching her swim laps. Now he stepped backward as she crooked an arm around the rim of the pool and pulled herself out of the water. She watched the late afternoon sun gilding the water's surface. "I love Todd, and he loves me," she said. "At least I think he still does."

Prince Albert barked.

"You're right," she said, wringing out her hair. "It's a silly fight. But I don't know how to end it." Elizabeth wished her mother was home; she could use some motherly advice. But both her parents were at a party at the Egbert house and would be gone for hours. Jessica should have been home by now, but she was late as usual. That left just Elizabeth and the dog. And Prince Albert wasn't offering any useful insights.

Elizabeth grabbed a towel and threw it over her shoulders, feeling the cool evening breeze raising goose bumps on her wet arms. The cordless phone rang on the poolside table. Excitement leaped inside her, and she snatched the phone, convinced that Todd had felt her thinking about him and decided it was time to apologize.

"Hello!" she blurted into the phone.

"Hi, Liz!" came Enid's voice.

"Oh, it's you."

Enid laughed. "That's quite a reception."

"Sorry, Enid. I was, uh, kind of hoping it would be Todd, calling to make up."

"Still no thaw in your own personal clique war? That's a bummer. I hate to see the two of you so miserable over this!"

"It all seems so dumb now," Elizabeth admitted. "So what if he's a jock and I'm not? So what if he thinks Tad was right to beat up on Nicky and I don't? We've disagreed about things before without splitting up over it."

"Everything gets more complicated when groups of people get into the act," Enid said. "Todd must be feeling a lot of pressure to show solidarity with his co-jocks."

Elizabeth nodded. "I never thought about it that way. But I know I've been resisting his side of things partly because I want to steer clear of being lumped into one of the cliques!"

"What do you want now?"

"I still don't want to be stereotyped," Elizabeth said. "But I do want Todd back!"

"Then call him!" Enid advised.

"I don't know, Enid. I mean, the phones work in both directions. It's not like he's made an effort to call me—"

"Somebody has to make the first move—"

The front door slammed, and Jessica's footsteps

clattered through the house. "Elizabeth!" Jessica screeched from inside. "Liz, are you here?"

Elizabeth sighed. "Jessica just burst into the house, and she's having a fit about something," she told Enid. "It's probably just her usual noncrisis of the week. But I'll call you back later, OK?"

Olivia stared in dismay at her computer screen. Sweet, sensitive Quarter was actually star football player Ken Matthews—the kind of guy who dated girls like Jessica Wakefield!

She'd been so excited about finding a soul mate, a boy who really seemed to understand her. Now her dreams had dissolved into reality. Olivia couldn't remember ever feeling so disappointed. Quarter was just a guy she'd seen almost every school day of her life and never paid much attention to.

"Oh, gosh!" she whispered, mortified by a new realization. "I even kissed him!" It had been a virtual kiss, but it had seemed so real—and so meaningful. And she'd shared so many intimate details of her thoughts, her hopes, and her dreams. She felt herself blushing furiously, wondering how she could face him at school Monday. At the same time her eyes filled with angry tears.

"You lied to me!" she accused, fiercely punching the keys.

"Not exactly," Ken typed back. "Nothing I said to you was untrue. Maybe I avoided a few subjects."

"A few subjects?" she keyed back, outraged. "Like your entire life!"

"I planned to tell you the truth," he said. "I was afraid of how you'd react, and I just never found the right time."

"How am I supposed to react? You pretended to be sensitive and poetic, but you're really a football player!"

"Oh, I see," he said. "This is more of that 'dumb jock' stuff I've been getting so much of at school. I thought you were the kind of person who would judge someone based on who he is inside! I didn't think you'd care about stereotypes!"

"I don't," she shot back. "But I do care about honesty!"

"Are you saying I'm not honest?" he typed in uppercase letters, so she'd know how angry she'd made him.

"What do you call it when you pretend to be someone you're not?" Tears were blurring the words on the screen, and she angrily wiped them away. "You led me on! Was it all a game to you,

Ken? Just another play on the gridiron?"

"I have to go figure out which side of the helmet goes in front," Ken replied. "You know how stupid we jocks are. See you at school."

His screen name blipped off the chat room roster, and Olivia was alone again—on-line as well as in real life. She gave her keyboard a shove and pounded her fists on her knees. She'd been right about one thing—meeting in person really had been the end for Freeverse and Quarter. But not for the reasons she'd feared.

"Elizabeth!" yelled Jessica, throwing open the door to her sister's bedroom. It was empty. She caught a glimpse of herself in the full-length mirror on Elizabeth's closet door. Her face was as white as her new shorts, and tearstains streaked her cheeks.

"I'm down here, Jessica!" called her sister's voice from downstairs. "I was out by the pool with Prince Albert."

Jessica ran to the top of the staircase. "Oh, Lizzie, I'm so glad you're home—"

"What is it this time?" Elizabeth interrupted in an exasperated voice as she began mounting the stairs. Elizabeth's hair was dripping. She wore her turquoise one-piece bathing suit and had a

187

thick towel wrapped around her shoulders. "Did Danny and Bryce get fed up with double teaming you?" Elizabeth asked. Then she looked up, saw Jessica's face, and froze. "Jessica, what's wrong?"

"Oh, Lizzie, it's so terrible!" Jessica sobbed. She slumped to a sitting position at the top of the stairs, her arms wrapped around her knees.

Elizabeth's arms were around her right away, and Jessica instantly felt safe and comfortable, even though her sister was damp and smelled faintly of chlorine.

"Did somebody hurt you?" Elizabeth asked, searching her face.

Jessica struggled to control her tears. "No, it's nothing like that."

"Where are Danny and Bryce?"

"They just dropped me off," she said, getting her voice under control. "They said they'd call the rest of the football team—"

Elizabeth shook her head, obviously mystified. Jessica felt a spray of droplets from Elizabeth's wet hair. "Call them about what?"

"Liz, we went by Blubber's house to see how he was doing," Jessica told her, "and there was an ambulance taking him away!"

Elizabeth gasped. "What happened? Is he OK?"

"We talked to the police, and they let us follow them to the hospital," Jessica said, clenching and unclenching her hands. She took a deep breath and looked at her sister. "Blubber tried to kill himself!"

"Oh, no!" Elizabeth breathed. "Will he be all right?"

"He took a lot of prescription pills his mother had around," Jessica said. "The police said they found him in time. Physically he'll be better in a few days."

Elizabeth blinked hard, as if to keep from crying. "Why would he do it? I know how upset he was about being suspended from the team. But to attempt suicide—"

Jessica shrugged. "It was more than that. Zack and a neighbor filled us in on some of it at the hospital, and we pieced the rest together."

"I remember that the guys on the team said Tad had been acting ballistic before the clique thing ever started," Elizabeth pointed out.

"It turns out Tad and Zack's parents have been having problems. Their marriage is on the rocks," Jessica said slowly, remembering a time months earlier when Mr. and Mrs. Wakefield had temporarily separated. "Their father moved out a few weeks ago."

189

"Poor Tad!" Elizabeth said, biting her lip. "He must have felt so alone."

"I just wish he had told somebody!" Jessica exclaimed, her voice trembling again. "Zack was too upset about it himself to be able to help his big brother much. But Tad's friends could have gotten him through it!" Prince Albert bounded up the steps and nudged her with his nose. Jessica hugged the dog gratefully.

Elizabeth stared at her fingernails. "Maybe you could have," she said slowly. "But I can understand why he didn't say anything. When it happened to us, I felt . . . *embarrassed,* even though I knew I shouldn't be. For a long time it was too painful to talk about."

"He was already upset about his family, and then he got in trouble for the fight with Justin at the dance—" Jessica said.

Elizabeth nodded. "And then half the school started treating him like a criminal," she said sadly. "Me included."

Jessica patted her arm sympathetically, hoping Elizabeth wasn't blaming herself for what had happened. "Zack says Blubber was throwing himself into football so he wouldn't think about his folks," she explained. "Getting kicked off the team must have been the last straw."

"This idiotic war of the cliques is at least partly to blame for this," Elizabeth said. "I never thought it would go so far!"

Jessica sighed deeply. "Nobody meant for it to."

"And now somebody has almost died!" Elizabeth exclaimed. "All because of some dumb posturing and petty rivalries!"

Jessica shook her head. "It's too late now, Liz. It's happened. It's history. We can't change anything."

"Yes, we can," Elizabeth said staunchly. Her voice sounded like a vow. "Are you OK alone, Jess? I need to make a phone call."

Jessica nodded. "Prince Albert will keep me company. Are you going to call Todd?"

"The fighting's got to end somewhere," Elizabeth said, rising to her feet. "It all seems so ridiculous now."

Ken's computer was turned off, but he sat staring at the dark screen. He wanted to punch its electronic face out. He spun away from his desk, pulled on his running shoes, and went out for a jog. Maybe the evening breeze would clear his head.

"Olivia Davidson!" he muttered to himself as he jogged down the sidewalk. He couldn't believe it. He'd fallen in love with an unseen poet whose words were full of mystery, romance, and magic. And it turned out to be just an ordinary girl—a girl he'd known since kindergarten without ever knowing her well.

That much he might have been able to handle, but then she went postal when she found out it was him—just because he was a football player! It wasn't fair. He was no Einstein, but he was as smart as anyone else. Why did people assume he was brain-dead just because he could throw a football? Why did Olivia think a football player couldn't possibly have a thought in his head beyond where the next touchdown was coming from? She didn't mind listening to his thoughts and dreams when she thought he was some kind of hippie.

"Suddenly she knows I'm a jock, so she thinks I must be a fraud!" he panted as he ran. "Like I've fooled her by pretending to have an IQ higher than my points-per-game average."

He knew now that he'd been wrong to consider dating somebody from outside his usual crowd. Obviously athletic girls like Jessica and Amy were the only ones who didn't stereotype jocks as having AstroTurf for brains.

Elizabeth pushed her damp hair behind her ear as she listened to the stunned silence on the other end of the telephone line.

"I'm shocked," Todd replied finally, his voice sounding small and very far away. "I don't know what to say."

"I feel that way too," Elizabeth said, wishing he was there with her, holding her. "Todd, I am so sorry for all of this!"

"It's not your fault," he said. "Blubber obviously has serious personal problems. You can't blame yourself for what he tried to do."

"In a way I am responsible," Elizabeth replied. "We all are. We all let these rivalries take over our lives. We let the differences between us become more important than each other. Even between you and me!"

"That doesn't matter now," Todd said, his voice coming across the phone full of emotion. "After this I think people will realize how far out of hand the clique wars have gotten. Nobody will have the heart to keep fighting."

"I know I don't!" Elizabeth exclaimed. "Todd, I am so sorry for the things I said about Tad— and about the rest of the football team. And about athletes in general, by extension."

"It's OK," he said. "We were both upset."

Elizabeth shook her head. "No, it's not OK. I didn't mean those things, and I didn't have the right!"

"And I'm sorry for the way I talked about some of your friends," Todd said.

"I was just feeling so insecure about not fitting in with the kids we spend time with," Elizabeth explained.

"Not fitting in?" Todd asked. "Where would you get that idea?"

"You were talking about sticking by your friends, the jocks," Elizabeth said. "I was afraid you'd be happier if I played team sports too."

"Aw, Liz, I didn't know you were thinking that way! I'm sorry I didn't see it. The truth is that I love you as much as ever. I wouldn't want you to be anyone but exactly who you are."

Elizabeth smiled, almost feeling the warmth of his hand around hers. For the first time in weeks she felt hopeful. "I love you too."

Chapter 13

Olivia slumped in a seat in the school auditorium on Monday as students filed in and scanned the room for places to sit. *Hundreds of kids are already in the room,* Olivia noted in her journal. *Yet it's strangely quiet, with only the hum of awkward, whispered conversations vibrating around me like insects.*

"He tried to kill himself!" Lila was whispering to Jessica and Amy in the row directly in front of Olivia. "That's as heavy as it gets! What possible good will it do for us to sit in the auditorium and talk about it with Chrome Dome?"

Amy shrugged. "At the Project Youth hot line they call it a crisis intervention. The idea is to tell everyone what happened—"

"As if every person in town hasn't heard the whole awful story a zillion times," Jessica interrupted. Olivia thought she sounded close to tears.

"Believe it or not, some people still don't have a clue about what went down," Amy told her.

"That might be a point," Lila agreed. "The jocks know about it, of course. But then there's the burnouts and the hippies and a lot of the others who have no life and never even talk to anyone remotely popular. They've got no other way of hearing the story."

"And anything they might have heard third- or fourth-hand is probably totally bogus," Amy said. "You know you can't trust gossip and rumors."

If Olivia hadn't felt so grim, she'd have laughed out loud. Amy Sutton was responsible for spreading more gossip and rumors than almost anyone in the junior class.

Lila thought so too. "You're the expert," she said dryly. Amy glared.

The whole school has seemed subdued all morning, Olivia scribbled. *Nobody knows what to say or how to act. For some people I think it's finally sinking in how stupid all the fighting has been. I know I feel terrible about Blubber, but I*

196

feel powerless. None of us knows how to move on and begin to build new connections.

"The other reason we're assemblying is to help come to terms with what's happened," Amy explained to Lila and Jessica.

"Assemblying?" Lila asked. "Let me guess— you plan to major in English in college."

"I was at Project Youth yesterday," Amy continued, ignoring the interruption. "And they're sending over some counselors today to talk to people about Blubber's . . . well, you know."

"Blubber's suicide attempt!" Jessica said, a little too loudly. Olivia saw a tear sliding down her cheek. "That's what it was, Amy! You can say the words!"

Lila patted her on the shoulder. "It's all right, Jess."

"No, it is not all right!" Jessica protested. "You two are carrying on a normal conversation, making jokes and giving each other a hard time like always. But one of our friends almost died! How can that be all right?"

"Of course it's not," Lila said. "All I meant was that Blubber's going to be OK."

"I know," Jessica said glumly. "And I'm sorry I lost it. I just wish I knew that the rest of us were going to be OK. Blubber tried to kill himself this week, but even that wasn't enough to change anything. Everybody's still mad at each other!"

Amy shook her head. "I don't think so. There haven't been any fights today, no graffiti, no dumb pranks—"

"It's a truce, maybe. But it's only temporary," Jessica warned. "Look around you! The jocks are sitting with jocks, the brains are sitting with brains, the burnouts are sitting with burnouts. It's just like last week."

Olivia glanced around her and saw that Jessica was right. At the end of Olivia's own row Justin and Jan were welcoming Nicky back to school. She was sure she saw Justin slip him a cigarette, which Nicky quickly slid under his jacket. Dana Larson sat a few rows behind Olivia with a group of body-pierced punkers with multicolored hair.

Jessica, for once in her life, has cut through the layers of prejudice and misunderstanding, Olivia wrote. *She knows the truth and it scares her—as it scares me. Today we have an uneasy peace. But no understanding. No resolution.*

Jessica continued. "All morning I haven't seen anyone—except Liz and Todd, thank goodness—going out of their way to talk to someone who's not in their clique," she said.

Olivia gazed around her again to confirm what Jessica had said. The first person she noticed was Bruce Patman, holding court across the aisle. As usual he was surrounded by student athletes, including his girlfriend, Pamela, as well as Danny, Bryce, Claire—and Ken.

Ken, she wrote in her journal. *There he is— tall, blond, and handsome—sitting on the outskirts of Bruce's soiree and staring intently at the back of the seat in front of him.* Olivia risked another quick glance, hoping nobody could see the flush she knew was spreading across her face. As far as she could tell, the quarterback hadn't noticed her at all.

Olivia had never had a one-night stand in her life, but she thought she knew now what it would feel like to share kisses with a guy for a night—and then wake up to reality and embarrassment the next day. But Quarter hadn't been a one-night stand. What they'd shared was a real relationship—or at least she'd thought it was. She shifted position so he wouldn't see her studying his profile from across the room. What did she really know about Ken?

I've known him forever, but I know nothing about him, she wrote rapidly, tuning out the girls' conversation in the row ahead of her.

Realization spread like a sunrise in her mind as she formulated her thoughts and recorded them at the same time. *All I've ever known about Ken is what I've assumed, based on the people he hangs out with. I've been stereotyping him as a dumb, superficial jock. But the Quarter who shared his thoughts with me wasn't dumb or superficial.*

"I'm the one who's been dumb and superficial!" she whispered, ashamed of herself. The only truly important things she knew about Ken were the things she'd learned on-line, when she was Freeverse and he was Quarter. After their covers were blown, she'd been nasty and cruel. She'd acted as if every idea he'd ever shared with her was suddenly invalid just because he played football.

For the first time Olivia admitted that she was as much to blame for the recent tensions as anyone else—maybe more, she told herself, since she was outside the cliques and should have been able to stay objective.

She sighed. *It's all a mess,* she wrote sadly. *I wish the real world were as clean and simple as the virtual one!*

As he waited for the assembly to begin, Ken tuned out Bruce's predictions about what

Principal Cooper might have to say. He'd been horrified when Danny had called him about Blubber on Saturday, and he still felt a sick, hollow ache inside when he thought about what his friend had been through.

Still, he couldn't help thinking about Olivia and kept catching glimpses of her through the shifting crowd in the auditorium, sitting alone. He'd never noticed before, but she really was cute—though not in the glamorous, perfect-featured, Hollywood sense that most people thought of as beauty. Nobody would put Olivia on a magazine cover, but she did have a distinctive style.

She seemed to be looking down at something in her hands as the students in the auditorium waited for the assembly to begin. Ken guessed she was either reading or writing. Or sketching, he thought, remembering that Freeverse had been an artist as well as a poet.

Freeverse. His own, special Freeverse was Elizabeth's friend Olivia. He still couldn't get over it. He thought back to the on-line conversations—the walks on the beach, the hikes and the poetry lessons, the cabin in the Rockies.

She'd been embarrassed to describe herself, he reflected with a weak smile. She said she was ordinary. She thought her hair was too crazy. He studied it now, thick and frizzy, gloriously free. He closed his eyes, and his fingers remembered. He'd run them through those soft curls, at least in cyberspace. He'd gazed into those big, hazel eyes, and he'd stroked the gentle curve of her cheek. And then he'd kissed her, and she'd kissed him back, while flames glowed orange on the hearth.

Mr. Cooper stepped onto the stage and tapped the microphone to check the sound, and Ken sighed gratefully. He couldn't allow himself to get caught up in those memories. The girl he'd fallen in love with didn't exist. He had to face that fact. It was too bad that Olivia hadn't turned out to be as wonderful and open-minded as Freeverse. But that's the way it was.

"It's over, man!" he whispered under his breath. "Let it go."

In the newspaper office after school that day Olivia sat on the couch and gazed thoughtfully at Elizabeth. "I think we're on the right track with this special *Oracle* issue," Olivia said, gesturing with the pages of an article she'd been editing for the arts section. "But it's not enough."

The piece in her hand was Maria's roundup of movies that might help students understand each other better, with suggestions for where to rent them and how to discuss them afterward. It was well written, and Maria's years in Hollywood made her an expert on films. But Olivia was beginning to think that words on newsprint couldn't begin to address the real problems at Sweet Valley High.

Elizabeth nodded. "I know what you mean," she replied, absentmindedly tapping her pen against the edge of her desk. "I've always been a big believer in the power of the press, but the situation at school has gotten too big and too depressing. It seems so unfixable." She opened a folder of completed stories for Friday's special edition and thumbed through them as if looking for one that might make a difference.

"We've all been talking as if there were no animosity among cliques until the night of that dance," Olivia said. "But things couldn't have spiraled out of control in one night. I think those tensions were already there, waiting beneath the surface for something to set them off."

"And that something was a silly disagreement about which music to dance to," Elizabeth said. "You're absolutely right about this beginning long before that dance. I don't know why I didn't look at it that way before."

Olivia lay back on the couch and stared at the ceiling. "No matter how great those articles are, they can't do more than give people something to think about."

"I used to believe that was enough," Elizabeth said. "But this time we don't have time to plant seeds in people's minds and hope they take root—"

"So everyone can grow a brain," Olivia finished for her.

Elizabeth laughed, but her eyes looked dull and anxious. "Besides, the newspaper doesn't come out until Friday, and it's only Monday now. We need to get people talking to each other—right now!"

After a minute of silently staring at a blank computer screen Elizabeth rose slowly to her feet and began pacing down the aisle between the computer workstations. "Three students have been physically hurt since that dance two weeks ago," she said as she walked. "Blubber would have died if his mother hadn't come home when she did!"

Olivia sat up. "And the tensions may have gone underground today, but they're still alive and well," she pointed out. "Who knows what will happen the next time a jock and a burnout go at each other?"

"Exactly!" Elizabeth said. "So what can we do—in addition to the special edition of the *Oracle*—to ease the tensions?"

"We need something that will get people involved and caring," Olivia said. "We need to get them talking to each other."

Elizabeth shook her head. "That sounds great, but we can't force people to talk to each other, let alone to understand each other. We need something that people will *want* to be a part of. Something fun. Something that can jump-start the healing process this school needs so badly."

Olivia crossed her arms in front of her, watching her friend curiously. "What do you propose?"

"I don't have a clue." Elizabeth shook her head. "I think I know what we need, but there's no practical way to do it."

"To do what? Do you have an idea?"

Elizabeth shrugged. "It's not exactly an idea; it's more of a pie-in-the-sky wish."

"Tell me," Olivia urged.

Elizabeth stopped pacing. "If only there was a way for us all to walk in each other's shoes for a while . . . ," she began. Her voice trailed off, and she resumed pacing across the office.

"You're right!" Olivia said after a moment's

pause. "We need a way to get people to talk to people they normally wouldn't socialize with." She thought about her on-line experiences and Quarter's, and she remembered how freeing—and how educational—it was to try on different backgrounds and personality traits risk-free.

Suddenly Olivia leaped to her feet. "That's it!" she cried triumphantly.

"That's what?"

"I've got it! I know exactly what we should do!" Olivia cried, her words tumbling over each other in her haste to get them out. "Grab a notebook, Liz! You and I are about to put together a plan."

Chapter 14

"You've gotten shorter!" Elizabeth said in surprise, gazing up at Todd as they danced in the crowded school gym.

"No, I think you've gotten taller," Todd said. "It must be the high heels."

Elizabeth giggled and looked down at the Italian sandals she was wearing. "I guess so! They're not much like my usual Keds."

"You're the one who said we had to walk in each other's shoes!" he reminded her. "Even if the shoes do have four-inch heels and all those skinny little strappy things."

Elizabeth and Olivia had dreamed up the "Walk in Each Other's Shoes" party as a fun way to get people to relax and start talking to each other. It was Saturday night, exactly three weeks after the disastrous dance that had put Justin in the hospital and touched off hostilities among the cliques. Now the students were gathered in the gym once more. But this time everybody looked . . . well, *different*. This time they were all walking in each other's shoes. Literally.

Elizabeth, for instance, was walking in Lila Fowler's shoes. And clothes.

"How can you smile so much while wearing torture chambers on your feet?" Todd asked, pitching his voice loud enough to be heard above the music, a peppy rendition of "In the Mood."

"I love these shoes!" Elizabeth insisted. She knew she sounded positively giddy, but she liked the unaccustomed feeling of letting loose. Something about putting on totally different clothes made her feel free to be a totally different person, like she could act any way she wanted. "In fact, I love everything about this night!" she raved. "We've got a fantastic turnout, everyone's having a blast, and I don't care how many blisters I get. I'm having a great time being Lila Fowler!"

"I hope you don't plan on applying for the job permanently," Todd said warily as the jazz standard

208

ended and a loud rap beat began pulsing from the speakers.

"Nope, it's a one-night engagement," she assured him. "At midnight the glass slippers disappear and the five-hundred-dollar dress turns into my orange nightshirt!"

The rule for party guests was that everyone had to wear something completely different from anything he or she would normally wear. All clothes and accessories had to be borrowed from somebody else at school. No buying was allowed.

Elizabeth stepped away from Todd and posed with a hand on her hip. She wore a meticulously tailored outfit of Lila's—a dress with a matching jacket in a soft shade of mauve silk with a coordinating hat, mauve nail polish, and more jewelry than she'd normally wear to a year's worth of parties combined.

"Looking good, Wakefield!" called Bruce Patman as he danced past them with Pamela in his arms.

"Wish I could say the same for you, Patman!" Todd yelled back. He and Elizabeth looked at each and burst into laughter. Bruce was wearing a short-sleeve plaid shirt that was too small for him, buttoned up tight and tucked into polyester pants. He was gazing at Pamela through horn-rimmed glasses, and he wore a pocket protector full of cheap plastic pens. A medal pinned to his chest said Math Competition Winner.

"Now there's an interesting new fashion statement from Bruce," Elizabeth said with a laugh.

"I'm more interested in looking at you," Todd replied, pulling her close for a kiss. He tugged on the black, oversize Loaded Chain Saw T-shirt he'd borrowed from Nicky. "What do you say, babe?" he teased. "When are you gonna come out on the smoking ramp alone with me? It's a very romantic spot, with all the smoke you can breathe and an unobstructed view of the trash cans."

"It's a tempting offer," Elizabeth said as they continued to dance. The music was rap, but they ignored the beat and danced slowly. She snuggled up against Todd's chest and thought about how wonderful it felt to be with him again and secure in his love.

After the rap song faded out, a slow, sad ballad swelled into the room. "The variety of music tonight is truly radical," Todd said. "It's like someone let a chimpanzee loose in a record store!"

"That's the idea," Elizabeth reminded him.

"You could've brought your own CDs if you wanted to hear anything in particular. And you know the rules—any music goes, dance like a maniac to anything, and no complaints allowed!"

"I'm not complaining," Todd said. "In fact, I think I like the inconsistency. Somehow it fits at this crazy party of yours!"

"Yes, it does," Elizabeth said. "I'm glad so many people responded to our requests for everyone to bring stuff from their own collections."

"How did Bryce end up playing DJ?" Todd asked. He pointed to the music table, where the clean-cut football player was wearing a Hawaiian shirt and big, baggy shorts.

"There wasn't enough time to book a professional," Elizabeth explained. "Bryce, Dana, and Winston each offered to take it for an hour. But come to think of it, I haven't seen Winston yet tonight," she realized suddenly. "Do you know if he's here?"

Todd shrugged. "I don't think he's arrived yet. He told me he'd be late."

Olivia ran up to them then, wearing a Sweet Valley High football uniform complete with shoulder pads.

211

"Number thirty-three," Todd said, reading her shirt. "That's Claire's jersey."

Olivia smiled. "I'm lucky we've got at least one football player whose clothes aren't too outrageously big for me!"

"It looks good on you, Liv," Elizabeth said. "Have you thought about trying out for the team?"

"Only if they decide to abandon football in favor of competitive Scrabble," Olivia said. "But isn't it awesome the way everyone is mingling? I had no idea we'd get this many people here!"

Elizabeth beamed, glad to see her friend so excited about the party. Olivia had been in the dumps all week. She hadn't wanted to talk about what happened at her date with the mysterious Quarter, but Elizabeth's guess was that he hadn't matched up to her expectations. Now, she thought, Olivia deserved to have a night of triumph.

"The great thing is that the mingling began days ago," Elizabeth reminded them, "since most people had to arrange to borrow clothes from kids they don't normally socialize with."

"And here are the two ladies who made it all happen!" called a male voice. Elizabeth turned to see Mr. Collins walking toward them in a Sweet Valley High basketball uniform. "Great job on this party, you two."

"I'm just glad that Chro—I mean, *Mr. Cooper* agreed to let us hold the party here as an official school function," Elizabeth said.

"It's exactly what this school needed," said the teacher. "Nobody expects one party to banish cliques and preconceived notions altogether. But it certainly casts the situation in a new light!"

"I'll say!" Todd remarked. "I never thought I'd see Justin Belson in a tuxedo! Did Bruce lend him his Porsche to go along with it?"

Mr. Collins laughed. "We'll save that for the 'Drive on Each Other's Wheels' party."

"The really wild thing is Justin's dance partner," Elizabeth said, pointing. "Check it out."

"*Lila?*" shrieked Olivia. "And she's wearing grunge! Now I've seen everything."

"I've also received a lot of compliments on yesterday's *Oracle* special edition," Mr. Collins said. "You girls and the rest of the newspaper staff should be proud of yourselves."

"Well, I'm proud of you," Todd said to Elizabeth. "For the newspaper and for this wacky party."

"Wacky is right!" Olivia said. "The sight of

213

Nicky Shepard dressed for Wimbledon is way weird!"

"And I see that Dana Larson left her nose ring at home," Todd said, pointing to the punk rocker, who was wearing an ultraconservative pin-striped business suit. "Though it's strange watching a punker in pinstripes do Texas line dancing to an old country-and-western song!"

"It's a surreal kind of night," Olivia said.

"I see Jan Brown and Amy Sutton are getting chummy over at the refreshments table," Elizabeth pointed out. "It could be the start of a beautiful friendship!"

"I never thought I'd live to see Jan 'Apathy Is My Middle Name' Brown in a cheerleading uniform!" Olivia said. "And what's even more amazing is that she's smiling!"

Mr. Collins watched the scene with quiet amusement. "Where have I seen that embroidered Mexican fiesta dress Amy's wearing?" he asked.

"On Rosa Jameson," supplied Olivia. "Her grandmother made it."

"It's really beautiful," Elizabeth said.

"Speaking of great taste in clothing, I really love your outfit, Mr. Collins," Todd told him, gesturing toward the basketball uniform. "I always knew you were a man of refinement and style."

"Wait a minute!" Elizabeth said, noticing the number on the jersey. "That's *your* uniform, Todd!"

"As I said, great refinement and style."

"You're not the only teacher who decided to dress for the occasion," Elizabeth told Mr. Collins. "I ran into Coach Schultz a few minutes ago. Have you seen him?"

"Not yet," said the English teacher, grinning expectantly. "Tell me more!"

"A cap and gown," Elizabeth said. "One of those really fancy, impressive ones like the Ph.D.'s wear to university ceremonies."

"This I've got to see!" Mr. Collins replied, a mischievous gleam in his blue eyes. "Besides, I have to check in with some of the other chaperons. Have fun! I'll see all of you later."

A few minutes after the teacher had left, Danny Porter appeared at Elizabeth's side.

"Jess—" he began. Then he blushed, staring at her face more carefully. "Sorry! Wrong twin."

Elizabeth shrugged. "In this outfit I'm not sure I'd recognize myself! But you make a pretty convincing hippie, Danny, for a wide receiver!"

"Have you seen Jessica around?" Danny

asked, idly fingering the fringes on his denim vest. "She promised me a dance."

"As a matter of fact, I just spotted her," Elizabeth said, craning her neck to get a better view of her sister. Suddenly the four-inch heels were becoming useful. "And with the way she's dressed, I'm surprised there are any guys left in the room who haven't already taken notice."

Jessica was decked out as a punker, in the same outfit Dana had worn to the disastrous dance three weeks earlier. She wore tight black leggings with a thick, studded belt and a skintight midriff top layered with a vintage bra of black lace, worn on the outside.

"Tell me Psycho Twin didn't get her nose pierced for this!" Todd groaned.

Elizabeth laughed. "It's a clip-on. And the tattoos are rub-ons."

"What a trip!" Olivia said.

Danny just stared, mesmerized. But after a moment his expression froze. A dark-haired boy appeared beside Jessica and was handing her a drink. Jessica reached up to kiss the boy, and he gazed down at her as if they were alone in the room. Elizabeth was sure she knew who the guy was, but the outfit confused her for a moment. He was wearing chinos, a button-down

216

oxford shirt, and an SVH letter jacket.

"*Keith Wagner?*" Danny asked, incredulous.

"You're right! That *is* Keith!" Elizabeth exclaimed. "He looks so . . . clean-cut!" She turned to Todd. "Wait a minute—don't I recognize that letter jacket? With Mr. Collins that makes two people who are running around in your clothes tonight."

Todd wiggled his eyebrows comically. "Keep watching," he advised.

"Who else?" Olivia asked.

"I'm sworn to secrecy!"

Danny's eyes were still fixed on Jessica. "She looks serious about him," he said forlornly. "I guess that explains why the last three tunes Bryce has played have been torch songs."

"Cheer up!" Todd said. "There's plenty of other girls here who'd be happy to dance with a jock-turned-hippie."

"Come on, Danny," Olivia said, holding out her hands. "How about a dance with a hippie-turned-jock? I promise I'll be gentle, seeing as you're on the rebound."

An hour later Olivia had danced with several other boys. Now she was thirsty and a little tired. It was time to hit the refreshments table at the far end of the gym.

Olivia had surprised herself by finding the courage to ask someone like Danny to dance with her, and she'd been just as surprised when he'd accepted. She'd always assumed that popular guys—athletes especially—wouldn't be interested in her. Now she wondered if her outsider status had been self-imposed, at least to an extent. Maybe cute, nice boys would have paid attention to her all along if she'd given them any encouragement. Maybe nobody really did care that she didn't feel at home in any one clique.

To be completely honest, she had to admit that she wasn't especially attracted to Danny. She'd asked him to dance on an impulse because he'd been so dejected when he finally realized Jessica wasn't seriously interested in him. But she had no romantic feelings for him, and she was sure he'd say the same about her.

For some reason the football jersey had made it easier for her to talk to a jock without wanting to sink into the floor. But in general she felt uncomfortable and awkward in the uniform, as if she was pretending to be something she wasn't.

Suddenly Olivia wondered if that was how Ken had felt, pretending to be sensitive and poetic for her. Then she shook her head. *There I am again, stereotyping him as an insensitive oaf just because he likes sports*. Maybe he always had been sensitive and poetic, and she'd been too blinded by his uniform to see it. Or, most likely, it was a little of each.

On the Internet she could relate to Quarter as a two-dimensional character in her own fantasy— a name on a screen. In the real world people were a lot more complicated than that because you had to deal with the whole person, not just the parts they wanted to let you in on. They had conflicting emotions, ulterior motives, and subconscious motivations. They had bad days, and they made mistakes. They were human. And it had been unfair of her to criticize Ken for being human. For not being the man of her cyberdreams.

She reached for a plastic cup of soda, but somebody else grabbed it at the same time. A tall boy in loose Guatemalan pants, a T-shirt, and Mardi Gras beads—the kind of outfit Keith Wagner might wear. Her eyes widened as she glanced up at the boy standing beside her. It was Ken.

Chapter 15

Jessica couldn't believe the transformation. She'd always thought Keith was cute. But now that he was dressed more Ivy League than third world, he was a major babe. And he hadn't even glanced at another girl in the last hour as they danced and talked together.

"It is so amazing to talk to someone who isn't all, 'first and goal' and 'a flag on the field,'" Jessica told him. "I think this is the first time in weeks I've had a conversation with a guy who didn't once mention the Raiders."

Jessica sensed a stir near the entrance to the gym, but she wasn't tall enough to see over the crowd. People were turning to look in that direction, and the noise level seemed to have inched upward.

"Speaking of football players, check that out," Keith said. The crowd parted, and Jessica saw who had just walked into the party. It was Tad Johnson and his brother, Zack. Both were dressed like burnouts—big, muscular burnouts, Jessica added mentally. Tad was holding a Hacky Sack ball in his hand. Zack clenched a cigarette, unlit.

Jessica grinned. "I'm glad Tad came tonight! And he looks good—well, except for the clothes, I mean. Other than that he looks totally normal!"

Keith searched her face. "Do you really like that dude?"

"He's my friend," Jessica said simply. "And he's going to have a tough time in the next few months. He'll need all his friends to stand by him."

"He'll have other people pulling for him too," Keith said. "I hear old man Collins has set up a study schedule to help the Blubmeister get those pesky grades back up."

"I didn't know that!"

"Collins is asking students to volunteer as tutors—even students of the nonjock variety."

"That's cool," Jessica said. "And the coach

told me there won't be any criminal charges from the thing with Nicky."

"Way to go, Blub!" Keith exclaimed. "I hope he can get his act together."

Jessica bit her lip. "Keith, how do you really feel about me and my friends? I mean, after everything that's happened, can you still say you hate jocks?"

Keith shook his head. "No, I'm cool with them. Live and let live, you know?"

"I'm glad to hear it," she said, relieved.

"Don't get me wrong!" Keith continued. "I'm not saying I plan to, like, invite Bruce Patman over tomorrow to meditate on my power crystals and listen to Joan Baez records."

"Now there's a truly bizarre mental image," Jessica said, laughing.

"No more bizarre than me wearing this getup from the Toddster collection!"

"You got the threads from Whizzer Wilkins?" Jessica asked. "They definitely look better on you than they ever did on him!"

Jessica gazed admiringly at Keith's broad shoulders, lean body, and piercing green eyes. There was something very appealing about Keith in any clothes. Sure, she'd dated him before and decided he was just too weird. And maybe that was still true. But then again, maybe it wasn't. Finding out one way or the other could be a whole lot of fun.

It took Ken a moment to recognize Olivia standing beside him at the refreshments table. He never in a million years would have thought of her in a football jersey. But it actually looked kind of cute on her. And he'd never noticed how pretty her eyes were in real life. She'd said they changed colors; today they looked golden brown, marbled with green.

"I'm sorry about your teammate," she said, blushing, after they greeted each other awkwardly. "I hope he'll be OK."

Ken fidgeted with his love beads. "I talked to Tad's brother this week. It sounds like Blubber is going to get the help he needs—for coping with his family problems and for learning how to control his temper."

"I'm glad," Olivia said sincerely. She hardly knew Tad, but she really did wish him the best. Nobody deserved what he'd been through.

"It's great that he was able to make it to this party tonight," Ken said, wishing desperately that he could think of something intelligent to say to her. "It's the first time he's seen anyone from school since—well, you know."

Olivia nodded. "Yeah. And it's good for everyone here to see him looking healthy and normal."

"If you can call the smoking-ramp fashion show 'normal' for a linebacker," Ken said with a laugh.

"I like your outfit," she told him. "You should wear that style more often."

"Olivia, can we go to the real-life version of a private chat room?" he asked. "Just for a minute?"

She blushed even pinker, but she nodded. Ken took her hand and led her to a relatively quiet corner. "I just wanted to say that I'm sorry I wasn't who you thought I was."

Olivia put up a hand as if to stop his apology. "It's not your fault," she said. "I should have expected that, meeting somebody on-line."

"I never wanted to mislead you," he said. "In all our conversations I never once said anything to Freeverse that I didn't mean completely."

She stared up at him, and again he was blown away by her big hazel eyes. "Thank you for telling me that," she said. "It means a lot for me to hear it."

"The truth is, you helped open up a part of

224

me that I never knew existed," he said, feeling a prickly warmth spreading over his face. "And whatever else happens, I'll always be grateful to you for that." Ken was acutely aware that he was talking in a way he'd never talked before, except for when he was on-line with Freeverse. He shook his head. "I'm sorry. I sound like a sappy greeting card."

Olivia touched him on the shoulder just for an instant. "No, you don't," she said. "You sound honest. And I think I know what you mean."

"You do?" he asked, relieved. *Most of the girls I know would be laughing hysterically by now,* he thought ruefully.

"I'm sorry too," she said. "I shouldn't have been so quick to judge you. I need to be more open-minded about people."

"We all do," Ken said, smiling down at her as his nervousness began to dissipate. "I guess that's what this party is all about."

"I really did have a wonderful time with you on-line," she said, returning his grin. Her eyes twinkled mischievously. "You know, Matthews— for a jock you have a poet's soul."

"Thanks, I guess," he said. "Just don't tell the guys on the team!"

"It'll be our little secret," Olivia promised.

"How about a real, actual, live and in-person, nonvirtual dance?" he asked.

Ken's hand on her back radiated warmth through Olivia's body as they danced to a Jamie Peters song. She liked his eyes. They were a warm, clear blue and were fringed with strikingly dark lashes for someone so blond.

The awkwardness between her and Ken was gone, replaced by real conversation like they used to have on-line. She suddenly knew they would be friends, and it was a good feeling.

As they danced and joked Olivia admitted to herself that she was attracted to Ken in a deeper way as well. After all, he was one of the best-looking boys at school—not to mention the star quarterback of the football team. A lot of girls were nuts about him. Olivia had never felt that way before, but now she was finally seeing him as an individual, not as one-eleventh of the human battering ram that was the SVH football team.

But she had to face facts. She, Olivia Davidson, was not homecoming queen material. After the rocky start she and Ken had just gotten past, she'd be happy just to be friends.

Suddenly somebody shoved her in the back,

and she fell against Ken hard. "Good thing I'm wearing shoulder pads," she murmured as she righted herself.

Oddly Ken burst into laughter.

Olivia turned to see who had nearly knocked her over. It was a person in a cheerleading uniform, with a V-necked sweater and a pleated skirt. The sweater had an *S* on the front, which could have stood for Sweet Valley, she supposed. But the uniform was purple and gold, not red and white.

She looked up at the clumsy cheerleader and did a double take. "*Winston?* Is that you?"

Ken was laughing so hard that tears were glistening in his eyes. Other couples on the dance floor were also starting to take notice.

"Sorry, Olivia," Winston said. "I didn't mean to barrel into you like that. I was late getting here, and it's almost my turn to take over as DJ, and—"

"What in the world are you doing in that getup?" Olivia asked.

"I could ask you the same," he said, squeezing her shoulder pads. "Methinks the lady's been pumping iron."

"You didn't follow the rules, Win!" she teased. "You were supposed to borrow your outfit from someone at school. You must have bought it somewhere. No way did you get it from somebody here!"

He made a show of fluffing his curly wig. "Way!" he said in a falsetto.

Olivia giggled. "Even if our squad had purple-and-gold uniforms, I know we don't have a cheerleader big enough to wear that!"

"Oh, yes, we do!" Ken sang out.

Olivia was confused. "Then whose cheerleading uniform is it?" she asked.

"It's Todd's!" Ken and Winston said together. They both dissolved into hopeless laughter.

"Exactly what do you guys do in that locker room of yours?" she asked.

Elizabeth and Todd joined them then, still holding hands, as they had been for most of the night. They looked amused at seeing Winston in drag, Olivia thought, but not surprised.

"Todd, Winston, and I bought cheerleading costumes so we could sneak into the big national competition to watch Liz, Jess, and Maria compete," Ken explained.

"They had a girls-only rule," Winston complained in his squeaky falsetto. "Highly discriminatory, if you ask me."

"What does the *S* stand for?" Olivia asked. "Sweet Valley?"

"Saskatchewan, actually," Todd said. "In our size ranges we couldn't be picky."

Olivia shook her head in disbelief. "So Winston, was your own cheerleading uniform just like this one you borrowed from Todd?" Olivia asked.

Winston turned up his nose. "Of course not, dahling. I had the formal version, as befitting my superior cheerleading skills and excellent hygiene."

"His had sequins!" Todd explained. "But your rules for the dance said all clothes had to be borrowed, so I let him wear mine instead." He turned to Winston. "But you know I want that uniform back in time for the next big game, Winnie!"

"No problem, Tilda!" Winston assured him.

"And I thought jocks were dull," Olivia said, still giggling.

"Speaking of jocks, you make a rather fetching one yourself, Olivia," Winston said. "I never thought of you as the shoulders-as-big-as-Texas type. But it works."

"Thank you, Winnie. You're a scholar and a gentleman."

"And a DJ!" he said suddenly, looking at his watch—which had a narrow gold band and rhinestones around the face. "A very late DJ. I gotta go play some music for you folks to dance to!"

A minute later a slow, romantic love song wafted from the speakers, and people paired off again. Ken smiled down at Olivia, and she melted into his arms. Nothing had ever felt as safe—and as exciting—as his strong, hard chest against her cheek. Her arms were around his neck, and she could feel tendrils of his blond hair as soft on her fingers as a kiss.

Ken took her chin in his hand gently and tilted up her face. "You're even prettier in person than you are on-line," he murmured, gazing into her eyes. Suddenly thoughts of romance between them didn't seem so far-fetched. "Would you like to go for another walk on the beach sometime?" he asked.

"A cyberbeach?"

"A real beach . . ." Ken's voice faded out, but his eyes still held hers, clear and blue. When he kissed her, his lips felt like raspberries, light as a whisper at first and then growing more insistent, more intense.

And Olivia knew there was nothing like the real thing.

BANTAM BOOKS TEMPT YOU TO TURN BACK TIME AND
DISCOVER A SECRET SIDE TO THE WAKEFIELD TWINS,
THE TRUTH! NEVER COMPLETELY KNOWN BEFORE –
UNTIL NOW!

SWEET VALLEY HIGH™

created by Francine Pascal

JESSICA'S SECRET DIARY

Jessica . . . the untold story

Dear Diary,
      I'm leaving home. I can't stand it anymore. Elizabeth
stole the man I love. I've lost everything to her. I hate being a
twin. I hate always being compared to perfect Elizabeth.
      Only you know, Diary, just how much she's taken from
me. After tonight, I'm sorry I went behind Elizabeth's back with
Jeffrey French. I'm not sorry about any of the things I did to her.
      Good-bye, Sweet Valley. From now on Jessica
Wakefield is going to be one of a kind!

Read all about Jessica's agonizing dilemma in this special edition
featuring classic moments from Sweet Valley High™ books 30 to 40.

The first volume of Jessica's tantalizing secret diaries.

ISBN: 0-553-40866-6

FANCY A PRIVATE GLIMPSE INTO THE DIARY OF
ANOTHER? READ ON . . .

SWEET VALLEY HIGH™

created by Francine Pascal

ELIZABETH'S SECRET DIARY

Elizabeth . . . the untold story

Dear Diary,

Todd and I are finished! I've never been more
miserable in my life. It all started when I found a letter on his
desk from a girl in Vermont. It sounded more than friendly, if you
know what I mean. I should trust Todd, but he didn't make things
better by getting mad at me for being a snoop (as he put it).

I know what you're thinking, Diary. I have no right to
complain. When Todd was gone, I let Nicholas Morrow kiss me. I
even fell in love with Jeffrey French. But Todd doesn't know the
worst. Only you, Diary, know the true story of what happened
between Todd's best friend, Ken Matthews, and me.

Read all about Elizabeth's steamy affair in this special edition
featuring classic moments from Sweet Valley High™ books 20 to 30.

The first volume of Elizabeth's tantalizing secret diaries.

ISBN: 0-553-40927-1

All Transworld titles are available by post from:

Bookservice by Post, PO Box 29,
Douglas, Isle of Man IM99 1BQ

Credit Cards accepted.
Please telephone 01624 675137,
fax 01624 670923
or Internet http://www.bookpost.co.uk
or e-mail: bookshop@enterprise.net for details

Free postage and packing in the UK.
Overseas customers allow £1 per book (paperbacks)
and £3 per book (hardbacks).